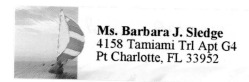
Through the Mists of Darkness

D1396721

Through the Mists of Darkness

a novel

Bonnie B. Robinson

Covenant Communications, Inc.

Cover illustration by Matthew Judd
Published by Covenant Communications, Inc.
American Fork, Utah

Copyright © 1994 by Bonnie B. Robinson
All rights reserved
Printed in the United States of America
First Printing: May 1994
94 95 96 97   10 9 8 7 6 5 4 3 2 1

Library of Congress Cataloging-in-Publication Data
ISBN 1-55603-693-7

For Colin, Erin, Quinn, and Ryan,
to whom I gave life, before giving life to this story.

"For thou wilt light my candle: the Lord my God will enlighten
my darkness."
Psalm 18:28

ONE

Lightning split the sky.

Startled, Jael grabbed a stone wall for support. The wind whipped her linen skirts and scattered debris over her sandals. Tightly gripping her shawl, she rushed on toward Uncle Nephi's, where her brother Seth had been staying.

The last four days had taken their toll on Jael, while she assisted Mother in midwifing for three women. The strain was far too much for Mother, who went to bed feverish, weeping that she missed Seth and wanted him at her bedside. Jael preferred to remain home to nurse Mother and to keep watch on their neighbor Hava, who was nearing the time of her travail. Yet Mother's dark-circled eyes pleaded with Jael to make the two-hour trek to Nephi's, despite the puffs of gray looming in the sky.

As Jael reached the city gates, the gale increased, thrashing her long, amber hair. She pulled the shawl over her head and hurried along the stone-slab highway into the center of Bountiful. Above her, storm clouds churned, tossing untamed thunderbolts. And a black vapor plunged toward the earth with a darkness so savage Jael shuddered.

Then the earth groaned and swayed beneath her. The highway heaved upward and burst, carving a chasm as far as she could see. A shriek caught in her throat. She turned and fled through a narrow passage. Roof tiles slid from housetops and shattered on the ground. Shielding her head, she rounded a corner to find a better route. Lightning sizzled so close she tasted it, dry and barbed on her tongue. As the quaking ceased, she reached her uncle's courtyard, where the wind stripped leaves off gnarled olive trees. Her lungs burned as she fought her way past the flailing branches to the stone house.

Jael beat upon the wooden door with white, tense knuckles. The sound seemed a whisper amidst the roaring tempest. She continued pounding, using both fists.

The door finally opened. Aunt Rachel drew her inside and shut out the storm. "Praise the Lord. He has brought you here in safety." Her ample arms circled Jael's quivering shoulders.

Aunt Rachel had cushioned many childhood fears. But at sixteen, Jael stood tall and awkward in the older woman's arms. Her nervous fingers kneaded Aunt Rachel's lamb's wool dress while wind-tossed branches scraped against the outer walls. Pulling away, Jael anxiously looked around the room. "Where is Seth? Mother has asked that I bring him home now."

"He is with your cousins in the next room." Aunt Rachel reached out to take Jael's shawl. "But I cannot let you leave in the midst of this storm."

She refused to give up her shawl. "Mother is in bed again with a fever, and her coughing stains her pillow with blood."

Aunt Rachel shook her head. "Poor Esther. She has endured many trials since your father died. And now, this lingering illness."

"While here in the city, I had thought to ask Zedekiah if he knows a better cure for Mother's cough than those we have tried."

Wind wailed through a shuttered opening in the wall. Jael glanced at the crack in the shutters to see lightning flash again and again, like mighty whips lashing the world.

"There is no better physician in the land than Zedekiah," said Aunt Rachel as thunder resounded.

A tremor shook the earth and rattled clay pots on the table. Jael's throat tightened. She had seen the highway sever at her feet. Was it even possible to get home? "Seth!" she cried, her voice hoarse with fear. "Come, Seth! We must hurry home."

"Please, abide with us a while." Aunt Rachel took Jael's hand and led her toward the hearth. The fire flared, then dwindled, as gusts blew down the smoke shaft to tease the flames.

Jael breathed in the aroma of the stew cooking in the hearth and wondered if Mother had eaten the soup she left at her bedside. "Where is Uncle Nephi?"

"He went to find more wood. When he returns, we shall inquire of him about your journey home. I only pray . . . oh, Jael, there have been countless signs and wonders. Would that you had brought Esther here with you."

"It is a two-hour walk—much too far for Mother to travel, even if we had a wagon or donkey." Rain splattered with fury in the courtyard. Jael twisted the corners of her shawl. "Aunt Rachel, I am filled with fear. Never before have I beheld a storm with such darkness. And never have I seen the ground tremble and split—" Her words were lost in a blare of thunder. She sank down upon a rough wooden bench beside the fire and bowed her head. Her nervous hands tugged at a strand of her amber hair. "Not a minute passes that I do not pray for Mother to be well again."

Aunt Rachel's soothing hands rubbed the tense muscles in Jael's shoulders. "Perhaps a blessing from Nephi will restore Esther's strength."

The door banged open. A slash of lightning snapped and lit the sky. Two young men darted across the threshold, followed by Uncle Nephi, who leaned his bulky frame against the door to shut it tightly. Thunder bellowed, vibrating the beams overhead.

The smell of damp forests followed Nephi across the room to the hearth. He set an ax and a bundle of logs in the woodbin. "The woes of heavy rains are upon us. But the Lord has provided us with enough dry wood to last for days." He motioned the young men forward with their heaping armloads. "Come now, you two!" He forced a laugh. "After nineteen years of eating like horses, you have finally learned to work like them!"

Though his words were light-hearted, Jael noticed that he lacked his usual joyful countenance. His clenched jaw caused the cords of his neck to protrude. And he kept glancing toward the door, as if his gaze alone might subdue the vicious storm. All the while, his strong arms unloaded and stacked logs, first from Jael's cousin, Jonas, then from the other young man. In the dim light, it took Jael a moment to recognize Jonas' friend, Mathoni, son of Zedekiah, the physician. She had not seen him for nearly two years, and his stature now surpassed Uncle Nephi's. His thick shoulders strained against the coarsely-woven tunic and deerskin vest. An orange headband circled his wavy brown hair and set off the warm tones of his tanned face.

"Mathoni has outdone you, Jonas." Uncle Nephi added wood to the fire. "He carried three more logs than you."

"Hah!" exclaimed Mathoni, nudging Jonas with an elbow. "I knew you had spent too much time reading those brass plates."

"To read the brass plates, you must be strong enough to lift them," was Jonas' mild reply. Jael saw that he was nearly as tall as Mathoni, but without the breadth. Like herself, Jonas had reddish hair and a rosy complexion, brought from Jerusalem to the Promised Land by their forefathers six hundred years before.

A thunderclap jarred the house. Jael gasped. Mathoni turned to see her. "Jael?" His left eyebrow cocked. "Is it truly you? I have not seen you since . . ."

"Oh, please!" Jael looked down to hide the rising blush as she recalled that day of feasting and dancing. It was the first time Mathoni's green eyes and broad smile had hinted of his interest in Jael as she performed a dance with the other women. Confused by his gaze, she soon spoiled the dance by tripping and falling into a portly man's lap. Mathoni had laughed at her awkwardness as she tried to free herself from the man's plump arms. Even now she heard a slight chuckle from Mathoni's throat. Her fingers nearly bored through her skirts. How she hated to be laughed at! Briskly, she stood and gripped her shawl closed. "I must go. Mother is alone."

Hailstones began pelting the house. Aunt Rachel took her by one elbow. "Jael, surely you . . ." A horrifying lament rose from the bowels of the earth.

Jael clenched her jaw as the mosaic floor rippled at her feet. The walls quivered, loosening the lime mortar between the stones. Clinging to Aunt Rachel, Jael's hands grew icy, and her mind froze as if a glacier had settled in. Only one instinctive thought remained: Get home to Mother. Yet the rampant quake kept her from acting on the thought.

As the jolting ceased, three boys rushed from the adjoining room: Seth and Samuel, who were half Jael's age; and little Amos, who toddled to his father's side.

Jael grabbed her brother's hand. Seth whimpered at the tense grip. Jael barely noticed. A chill swept like a blizzard over her flesh. She turned stiffly toward the door and reached for the wooden latch.

But Uncle Nephi seized both Jael and Seth and brought them again to sit beside the fire. A power shone in his face as he spoke. "You must not leave. The fullness of the wrath of the Lord is upon this land. The time for repenting has passed. I have witnessed the highways breaking up and seen the mountains beginning to fall. It is just as Samuel prophesied."

"What did I prophesy?" asked Samuel.

"Not you!" Jonas picked up his little brother and hugged him against his chest. "Samuel, the Lamanite prophet. He prophesied to the Nephites about this mighty storm."

"This 'Almighty' storm," corrected Uncle Nephi.

"Let me go!" Samuel tried to push away. Jonas bent over and set him on the bench beside his cousins. "But Father," Samuel persisted, "I thought you were the prophet and high priest. How could a Lamanite be a prophet?"

"Anyone who is called by the Lord . . ." Uncle Nephi's words were drowned as the wind hurled hailstones against the roof. A murky vapor seeped through cracks in the house made by the earthquake. Despite the extra logs on the fire, the room darkened.

Jael wrung the edges of her shawl. "Oh, please, Uncle Nephi! What about Mother? There is no one to care for her."

Uncle Nephi knelt and looked directly into Jael's eyes. "My brother Timothy is quick to visit your mother in times of trouble. But more important, Jael, you must remember that the Lord is mindful of her. Perhaps we should unite in prayer for Esther's safety." Uncle Nephi bowed his head, and waited for others in the room to bow theirs.

Jael tried to concentrate on her uncle's solemn prayer. The wind howled and battered the house, as if mocking his every word. Jael pressed her folded hands against her heart and searched for the seeds of faith planted there at an early age. But all she found was fear, plowing her faith asunder.

Uncle Nephi rose from his knees and patted Amos' head, which rested upon Aunt Rachel's shoulder. "Perhaps we should read from the prophecies of Samuel the Lamanite. Jonas, will you get the plates of Nephi?"

"Yes, Father." Jonas strode across the room to a large stone box at one end of the table.

Uncle Nephi took an oil lamp from the mantel, then knelt to light it with a stick from the fire. A sudden wind hissed down the smoke shaft, scattered the ashes, and nearly doused the flames. Uncle Nephi choked as thick smoke swirled into his face.

Mathoni's left eyebrow raised. He crouched beside Nephi, took the lamp, and carefully lit the oil. "Thank you," Uncle Nephi sputtered, still clearing his throat. He wiped the soot from his face with a cloth, then settled on the stone hearth near Aunt Rachel's feet.

Jael studied Mathoni's generous features as he folded his

cloak and tucked it under his brawny arm. Then he sat cross-legged at the opposite end of the hearth. The resolute lift to his chin showed he was undaunted by the tempest, and Jael longed to borrow his fearlessness for her journey home. Concern for Mother knotted in her stomach like the corners of her shawl knotted by her taut hands. "Would that you could keep your hands still," Mother had often said. "Forever moving, forever flitting about." Jael forced her hands to stay folded in her lap.

Jonas came forward, laid open the heavy metal plates before his father, then sat beside Mathoni. Uncle Nephi began to search the plates. "We are blessed to have the word of the Lord so close at hand."

Jael concentrated on the clink of turning pages—anything to distract her from the fierce storm and her worries about Mother. At least the ground had quit shaking, she thought.

As if her thought were audible, the earth surged violently again. Ceiling beams creaked and popped. She covered her head in case they fell. Then the floor buckled with such force that the bench overturned, flinging everyone to the floor.

"Oh, please!" Jael cried. But her words were lost in the profound rumble as the world tore itself apart. The room lurched and reeled. Wooden plates rattled to the floor. A rafter fractured and fell, inches from Seth's head. Jael pulled him closer and buried her face in his hair to keep from screaming. Her hands clenched his coarse tunic until her knuckles ached.

Nearby, Amos whimpered in his mother's arms. "Hush, dear one, hush," Aunt Rachel soothed. Finally, the upheaval ended, though the hail and thunderbolts raged on. Aunt Rachel touched Jael's hand. "Are you all right?"

Jael couldn't speak around the tears in her throat, but she squeezed her aunt's fingers. Then she sat up and looked at Seth. A gash on his forehead had stained her shawl with blood. "Oh, Seth! You are wounded."

"I bumped my head when I fell." He pointed to the beam

which had dropped from the ceiling. "At least that missed me."

"It almost hit me!" exclaimed Samuel. "Then we would both be dead!"

"Hush!" said Aunt Rachel, handing Jael a cloth to hold on Seth's wound. Then she pushed the bench aside, slid over beside Nephi on the floor, and drew Amos onto her lap. She smoothed back the toddler's pale hair, kissed his brow, and looked into her husband's somber eyes. "Please, read to us."

The oil lamp in Uncle Nephi's hand was out, and the fire waned. Mathoni stirred the embers with a stick, set on some twigs and another log, and fanned the small flame into a blaze.

Jael checked Seth's wound. The bleeding had stopped, and she set the cloth aside. Yet she could not set aside her need to get home. She rubbed her nervous hands together. Even if Uncle Timothy and the Lord were mindful of her, Jael had to see for herself that Mother was all right.

She was also determined to find a cure for Mother's stubborn disease of the lungs. Perhaps while there, she would confer with Mathoni, an apprentice physician under his father's tutelage. Then, no matter how sinister the storm nor the danger to herself, she would muster the courage to journey home.

Thunderbolts shattered the momentary stillness. A shiver raced up Jael's spine. She tucked her skirts around her legs for warmth against the mosaic floor.

Uncle Nephi began to read. "'And behold, again, another sign I give unto you, yea a sign of his death.'"

"A sign of whose death, Father?" asked Samuel.

"Jesus Christ, the Son of God." Uncle Nephi ran his fingers across the engravings on the metal plates as he continued. "'Yea, at the time that he shall yield up the ghost there shall be thunderings and lightnings for the space of many hours, and the earth shall shake and tremble.'"

Jael's mouth went dry. She had heard Uncle Nephi read this from the pulpit in the synagogue. Now it suddenly rang true, hauntingly true. She clenched her hands into fists and pressed them against her forehead. "Get home to Mother! Get home to Mother!" echoed in her mind. But fear anchored her to the floor.

As wind bawled through cracks in the shutters, Uncle Nephi raised his voice. "'And behold, there shall be great tempests, and there shall be many mountains laid low, . . . and many highways shall be broken up, and many cities shall become desolate.'"

"Desolate?" Seth interrupted. "What does that mean?"

"Empty," answered Jonas. "Without people."

Uncle Nephi's words clashed against the chaos outside. "'Behold, in that day that he shall suffer death the sun shall be darkened and refuse to give his light unto you; and also the moon and the stars; and there shall be no light upon the face of this land, even from the time that he shall suffer death, for the space of three days, to the time that he shall rise again from the dead.'"

"Three days?" Mathoni's deep voice cut through the storm.

"Three days," confirmed Jonas with a nod of his head. "Perhaps *you* should have spent more time reading the plates along with me."

"Me?" bellowed Mathoni as his left eyebrow shot up again.

"'And the angel said unto me that many shall see greater things than these, to the intent that they might believe . . .'"

An army of thunderbolts exploded. Jael pressed her clammy fingers against her ears, but the sound blared on until her head buzzed.

A pair of powerful hands tugged her to the floor. "Lie down!" commanded Mathoni's husky voice. He cushioned her head with his folded cloak. "I have often seen valiant soldiers pass out, and it is not pleasant."

Jael pulled Seth beside her and curled around him. Lightning cracked in the yard. A massive tree branch broke through the roof and crashed upon the table. The lightning had lit the branch with fire! Mathoni snatched his cloak from beneath Jael's head and raced over to beat back the blaze. Jonas and Uncle Nephi quickly joined him, pounding on the flames. Hail poured through the hole in the roof, aiding their efforts to douse the fire.

Then a deafening roar encompassed the room, as if the whole house might cleave apart. The floor heaved upward, upsetting large clay jars, which burst and spilled their contents. Chunks of stone cracked off the tilting walls. Shutters tore from their hinges and slapped against the floor. And the cruel gale spit its way inside, spewing hailstones everywhere.

Jael screamed and clung to her brother with all her might. Beneath her shoulder, she felt a crack sever the mosaic floor. Another fissure sliced the wall beside the hearth, then split the ceiling. Two more rafters fell in the corner near the table. One caught Uncle Nephi's shoulder, and he yowled in pain.

As the earth continued to gyrate, more crevices opened in the walls and roof. Then, through every crack, a malicious black vapor slithered in, bringing the dense smell of smoke. The repulsive vapor crawled forward and enveloped Jael. She could hardly breathe. She pulled the shawl over her mouth and nose to filter the venomous air.

Thick as tar, the black mist plunged through the hole in the roof. The tree branch vanished from her view. So did the three men. Spiraling forward, the dense fog saturated Jael with fear. It drenched her clothing, sickened her stomach. One by one, Aunt Rachel and her cousins were buried in blackness.

All that remained were a few blood-red coals in the hearth. Jael struggled to keep them in sight. She felt the burden of her brother, lying still—too still—in her arms. She shook him. She tried to speak his name. But the vapor congealed in her throat and made her cough.

The embers sputtered and drowned in the black mist. Jael writhed as the vapor seized her and crushed her lungs like a massive weight. It forced her to let go of Seth. It grappled with her and told her to quit breathing. She strained against the press of death. She fought to inhale just one small breath of air.

The blackness solidified. Jael became part of it. And all was dark.

TWO

A cough awakened Jael—deep in her throat. Her cheek lay pressed against the cold mosaic floor. She raised her head slightly and opened her eyes. Nothing. The black vapor enshrouded her like a wet blanket. She closed her eyes and wondered if this was how death felt.

Yet she was not dead. Her lungs ached with each intake of the pungent vapor. And her heart pulsed faithfully, getting faster with each new thought: Time. How much had passed? Thick darkness. Or was she blind? Quiet. Had she survived while everyone else died? Her skin prickled.

Stretching out a shaky hand, she touched the motionless form of her brother. "Seth." She gagged on the mist that filled her throat. "Oh, please, Seth, wake up!" She pulled him close. He was cold, but not lifeless. She rubbed his arms and legs, trying to warm them. He stirred and began to revive.

"Jael?" he whispered. "Where are you? I cannot see you."

"Nor I you. But I am here beside you."

"Where is Samuel, and Uncle Nephi, and everyone?"

"I wish I knew." Jael raised up on one elbow, but it was useless looking across the room. "Aunt Rachel?" she ventured.

"Jael, is that you?" Her aunt sounded far away.

"Are you all right?" asked Jael.

"Yes, dear."

Jael sat up and pulled straggles of hair off her face. Still nothing came to view. But she heard a voice moan in pain. Instantly, she remembered Mother. Jael bolted to her feet and took two steps. The overturned bench caught her ankle. She sprawled on the damp floor.

"Jael!" Seth cried. "Stay with me!"

"Aunt Rachel shall take care of you. I must go to Mother." Once more, she got to her feet and shuffled forward to find the door. Moving through the heavy vapor was like moving through quicksand, and it felt thick and noxious in her lungs. Yet somehow she reached the door and groped for the wooden latch. Her hand touched another hand! She jumped back and nearly stumbled again. She felt a firm arm across her back, as a deep voice said, "We shall speak when we are outside." The door scraped open, she was propelled forward, then the door slammed shut behind them. They moved a few steps from the house. "It was important to hurry out before Nephi changed his mind about letting us leave." Jael now recognized the voice as Mathoni's. She squinted, trying to see him in the darkness. "We shall have to move slowly," he warned. "I believe that a tree in the courtyard has fallen. And who knows what else we may find?"

With his arm thrusting her forward, Jael had little choice but to inch through the darkness. Her arms swam before her, trying to part the dark fog and search for obstacles. As she panted in fear, the smoky vapors churned through her mouth and nose. Mud oozed around her sandaled feet. Her arm hit a branch.

"Just as I thought." Mathoni's hands circled her waist. "Let me help you over the fallen tree."

"I can do it myself." Jael twisted from his grasp, hoisted her skirts, and climbed on the large trunk. The bark, coated with hail, was slippery and cold. As she slid down the other side, her skirts snagged and ripped.

"Hah!" Mathoni landed beside her. "You should have let me help you."

Laughing at her again! She tugged furiously at her skirts to loosen them from the limb where they were caught. Behind her in the house, Amos wailed. Down the street echoed another child's cries. Then other voices, young and old, began to moan and weep. Jael was paralyzed by the eerie howlings.

Mathoni reached over to free her tangled skirts. His hand brushed hers and lingered there a moment before unsnagging the fabric. "Now, if we only had a torch to light our way."

His words brought Jael back to her task. She smoothed her skirts into place. "Yes, we need a torch. Can we not go back and get one?"

"It is no use. Nothing will catch fire. This vapor is nearly as thick as the mud at our feet."

"What about an oil lamp?"

"Jonas tried that. Then he quoted Samuel's prophecy about the three days of darkness and set the lamp aside."

"I thought it was only the sun, moon, and stars that would be darkened."

"'No light upon the face of this land' is what the scriptures said. I almost wish we had not beat out the flames on the branch that broke through the roof." Jael heard a sharp snap. "In the meantime, we shall have to use another means to find our way." From the sound, Mathoni was stripping a limb of twigs and leaves. Then he rapped it on the ground. "This will serve as our guide." His free arm anchored behind her waist.

"Our guide?" she asked, uncertain of his plan.

"To help us find our way to your home." Before Jael could respond, his arm again thrust her forward. Her hands combed the perilous vapor while her feet struggled over fissures and fragmented stones. Repeatedly, her skirts caught on debris, and sudden limbs lashed her arms or whipped her face. She squeezed her eyes shut. They were useless. And this way she could restrain the searing tears that welled beneath her eyelids.

From the blackness came an increasing lament of voices. "Oh, that we had repented," groaned one man. "Forgive our sins, Lord, save us from this darkness!" wailed another. "Levi, where are you?" cried a woman. Others merely wept and sobbed. The earth shook repeatedly, as if in response to their howlings.

Jael's head reeled from the endless babble and quaking. With each step further into the unknown, her courage waned. She dragged her feet, becoming more vulnerable to shattered rocks and rubble, which stabbed through her sandals. A ghastly odor hung like wet smoke in her lungs. She smelled burned timbers, burned cloth, and burned flesh. Fear curdled in her veins, making her pulse sluggish. The only certainty now was in the firm grip of Mathoni's arm at her waist. She wondered why he would venture out with her into the carnage. "Mathoni, why did you come?"

He failed to respond to her question. Halting his footsteps, he let go of her. "Wait here," he said and tapped quickly away, leaving her without a thread of security.

Jael mouthed his name. But no sound came from her throat. She gripped her neck with both hands, trying to loosen the bands of fear. She could barely breathe, so thick was the black mist that saturated her with its deathly stench and chill. And all around, people wailed in deeper anguish. Soon, the taut grip of her fingernails drew blood from her own neck. Then nearby, she heard a clatter, a crack, a reverberating boom, and someone screaming.

No longer could Jael stand there alone. With jittering hands, she found her way along a stone wall, moving in the direction Mathoni had tapped away. Feeling her way along the wall, she reached a place of crumbled stone, where it came to an end. Her whole body drooped in despair. "Oh, please!" she said weakly. "Mathoni, come back." Waving her hands before her, she gradually moved forward. Then one knee struck a timber, and she wailed in pain—her voice merging with other cries.

"Jael?" Mathoni called. "Jael, where are you?"

"Here," she said, not much above a whisper.

"Are you all right?" The tapping of his stick came nearer.

She drew in a shuddering breath. The bands of fear loosened

from her throat as Mathoni reached her side.

"Why did you not wait where I told you?"

"I hurt my knee. I stumbled against a timber. I could not bear to—Oh, Mathoni! Why did you leave me alone?"

"A timber? Where is it? We might need it for prying things out of our way."

Jael straightened up and put her hands on her hips. Her remaining fears ignited into anger. Mathoni did not seem to care that she was hurt. Nor that she had feared being left alone. She grabbed his hand and thrust it toward the timber. "Here!"

What they found was stiff. But it was not a timber. "Hah!" Mathoni laughed. "It is the leg of a horse! A very dead horse."

Jael caught her breath. A bitter taste rose in her throat. She tried to swallow it away, but it lodged at the back of her tongue. Her stomach clenched. She gritted her teeth and swallowed again. But the nausea continued to consume her.

"This way." Mathoni once again forced her forward with his arm behind her waist. "I have found a passageway that leads up the hill. I hope it is clear of debris."

The passage was narrow. Jael felt her way along mud bricks, stone walls, then more bricks and more stone. Her fingers jammed against a protruding stone. She winced and bit her lip against the pain, while Mathoni urged her slowly onward. Soon her knee began to throb.

The mists of darkness seemed to sap her strength and slow her down, as if she were caught in a slimy net. She listened to the cries of others who were also trapped in the reeking black haze. "So many cries of anguish," she said weakly. "They make my heart feel sad and hollow."

Mathoni jerked her to a halt, but he said nothing. She heard the stick tapping, higher and higher until it stopped above her head. "Are you able to climb a pile of rubble?"

Her final bit of stamina vanished. She buried her face in her hands. "Oh, please, Mathoni! I am far too weary."

"Jael, are you crying?" His voice was more sympathetic than she expected. "What is there to cry about?"

She leaned her back against a rough stone wall and let sobs shake her shoulders. There was plenty to cry about.

"Come now, Jael. Stop your crying. It is not necessary for us to climb the rubble. We can find a different passageway."

"My house is on the far side of the valley, near the river."

"I know." Mathoni leaned against the wall beside her.

Jael sniffled. "Why did you leave Uncle Nephi's?"

"For the same reason as you. I have a frail mother to look after. Also, my father is elderly and my brother is crippled." He paused, as thunder roared in the distance, then added, "At least I received consent from your uncle before leaving."

Jael pressed her hands upon her aching heart. Uncle Nephi had been so good to her over the years. Yet she had not stopped to talk with him, even after she saw the rafter wound him as darkness engulfed the world.

Mathoni must have guessed her thoughts, for he said, "The fallen rafter broke Nephi's shoulder. I straightened the bones and bound them with a strip of cloth."

"Was he in much pain?"

"Enough that he allowed you to slip from under his watchful eye." Mathoni cleared his throat. "Had I not promised to see you safely home, do you think they would have let you leave?"

Jael shook her head, forgetting he could not see the motion. "Was everyone else all right?"

"Yes. Rachel made sure of that. After checking that you and the boys were still breathing, she felt her way along the floor toward me and Jonas. She offered her sash to bind Nephi's shoulder. I had just finished wrapping it and decided to leave when we heard you talking with Seth. So I waited for you at the door."

Jael blotted her tears on the corner of her shawl. "What chance is there that my mother is still alive?"

"Or mine?" Mathoni asked, echoing her sadness.

THREE

Jael drew in a deep breath, then coughed against the noxious mist that filled her lungs.

"Many are still alive," Mathoni said. "Their cries are all around us."

"If we cannot cross the city to reach your house, how can we cross the valley to reach mine?"

"I have faced numerous hosts on the battlefield more hostile than this darkness." Mathoni paused, then added, "As a physician, my greatest foe is death. I suppose it is everyone's worst enemy."

"To some, death is a bless . . ."

The earth began to shake, pulverizing the wall behind them. Mathoni yanked Jael's arm and dragged her back through the passageway. Each step bruised her sandaled feet. Dust and debris splattered in her face. Her injured knee ached. "Wait! Please stop," she begged, but her words vanished in the clamor.

Mathoni continued to impel her along until the vibrations ceased. "Good," he said. "Are you all right?"

"Yes," Jael panted. "Yes." She had no idea how far they had run nor where they might be. In the bitter blackness, she wondered if Mathoni knew.

His stick began to tap, first right, then left. "This way."

"Oh, please. I must rest."

"Rest at my house. It is but a short distance away."

"How can you be certain?"

"Hah! I know where my house is. I have lived there all my life!" His muscled arm fastened around her narrow waist. "Someone needs to do a better job of feeding you. So while you rest, I shall fix us both something to eat."

Jael forced her feet to slide along, though she ached with exhaustion. Stones and rubble pricked her feet. Foul odors from smoke and singed flesh sickened her stomach. Tree branches slapped her arms and face. Sad voices lamented in the darkness, haunting her heart. She leaned more heavily against Mathoni.

As the ground rose up a hill, a numbness overtook her senses. The tapping stopped, and Mathoni slowed her to a halt. "Everywhere we turn there are heaping piles of debris. Somehow we must get over them to reach my house."

"I shall climb," breathed Jael, dull of feeling.

"Hah! You are so weak you can barely stand."

Her pulse quickened. That he could laugh at her in the midst of this chaos provoked her into action. She knotted her shawl securely at her neck. Then she leaned forward and touched the musty-smelling rubble. Mud bricks, clay roof tiles, upturned earth, bushes, rocks, linens, pottery, drinking gourds, furniture—she felt it all as she gradually scrambled upward.

Beside her came the rasp of Mathoni's breathing as he also ascended the bulky pile. "I cannot wait to see this destruction when the three days of darkness are passed," he puffed.

Jael did not respond. She was too busy biting back the pain from crawling on her swollen knee. She longed to stop. But concern for Mother made her continue reaching, grasping, creeping forward. Soon the pile descended. She moved downward, clinging to whatever her searching hands could grasp. Suddenly, the weight of her body loosened the pile. She began to slide and scream.

"Jael!" yelled Mathoni. "Strive to catch hold of something."

She grabbed a narrow timber, but splinters of wood pierced her hand, so she let go and continued falling. Debris scratched her arms and legs as her body jarred its way down the pile. Her skirts and shawl ripped again and again. The wreckage jabbed at her back, then her chest, as she tumbled downward.

Finally, it was over. She landed on something soft. Something that felt like cloth. Cloth with flesh underneath. Cold, lifeless flesh. She bolted to her feet and stumbled through the black mist. Her ankles twisted and throbbed from the uneven ground. Bushes tore at her clothing and clawed her face. Soon she fell, knocking out her breath. The ground where she lay was muddy, and the moisture quickly penetrated her clothing.

Mathoni's voice blared through the blackness, "Jael? Jael? Where are you?" His footsteps drew nearer, but she was too dazed to speak. "Jael! Please tell me where you are."

Her chest convulsed, trying to regain air. She coughed, gasped to fill her lungs, and coughed again.

In an instant Mathoni was at her side and endeavored to raise her. "Get up! Your clothes are drenched." He gently grasped under her arms and lifted her up. "What were you thinking, going off by yourself? You shall be no good to your mother lost . . . or dead."

"Forgive me," she scarcely said.

"Help us!" came a faint cry. "Please, help us!"

"Is someone there?" called Mathoni.

"Yes! Will you help us?"

Mathoni patted Jael's shoulder. "We should go help them."

Jael shivered. Her taut hands clenched the damp shawl at her neck. She hung her head. She searched within. There was nothing left. No stamina, no strength—nothing to give her the courage for one more step into the dark dangers surrounding her.

Mathoni tugged on her arm. "Please come, Jael. Helping someone else will keep our minds off our own troubles."

Jael finally began to move, dragging her feet in the spongy soil. Mathoni's strong arm at her waist became the only warm spot on her drenched frame. Her muddied skirts hung heavily, weighing her down. Yet the cold moisture on her knee soothed the swelling, allowing her to walk with less pain.

"We are coming!" Mathoni called in the direction they had heard voices. "Keep talking so we can find you."

"Here! This way. Please help us!" shouted a mingle of mature and childish voices, filled with grief.

"What help do you need?" Mathoni steered Jael around an unknown hazard that his stick found.

"My husband is pinned under a pillar from the porch of our house. My children and I are all right, but we have not the strength to move the stone pillar."

"A stone pillar?" asked Mathoni. "Who in the land has stone pillars on his porch except the chief judge?"

"My husband is the chief judge, Hosea," said the woman as her children wept nearby. "I am Deborah."

"And I am Mathoni, son of Zedekiah, the physician."

"Mathoni! You are an answer to our prayers."

"I have come into your courtyard. Is the porch to my left?"

"Yes," Deborah answered. "We are at the corner of the porch farthest from you."

Once more the earth jolted beneath their feet. Weak and chilled, Jael clung to Mathoni while the tremor rattled through the courtyard. A horrid odor punctured the darkness. Jael's stomach tightened. Finally the earth quit shaking.

"Is Hosea conscious?" Mathoni asked.

"He is awake. But he has suffered much pain."

"Please help us," a child cried. "I do not want my father to die!"

The child's plea flooded Jael's heart with empathy. She pushed her fatigue aside and called, "We are coming."

"Is someone with you, Mathoni?" asked Deborah.

"The Prophet Nephi's niece, Jael." For a moment he let go, and Jael sensed he was groping in the darkness. Then he reached for her arms and eased her downward. "Here. Sit on the porch steps while I go see what I can do."

"I want to help," she said in a weak voice.

"Hah!"

"I am not as useless as you think," she said, daring him to laugh at her again. "Perhaps I could tend the children to keep them out of your way."

"Fine," Mathoni said as he moved away.

"Deborah," called Jael, "send your children to me on the porch steps, and I shall tell them rhymes and stories."

"Dinah, take your brothers and sister to sit beside Jael."

She heard Deborah kiss several of the children before sending them off. Then kneeling, Jael reached through the blackness to find them. "This way," she said, hearing their whispers and shuffling feet. "Reach out and take my hand."

"Thank you, Jael," said their mother. "They have been hovering over their father and praying for a long while."

"There!" Jael snatched the first small hand. Then five children crawled up beside her. Their clothing was as damp as hers, so she welcomed the two smallest into her lap while the others huddled tightly against her side. "Would that we had a fire," she said, cuddling the children for warmth.

"We tried to start one," said the oldest, who Jael assumed was Dinah. "But we could not get it to light."

Hosea began to moan, making the children shiver all the more. "Oh, that we had repented," he wailed, "before this great destruction came upon us."

"The house of Hosea has no need to repent," Mathoni said in a soothing tone. "Please lie quietly and rest."

Jael heard Deborah sob, "Will he be all right?"

"Yes," answered Mathoni. "His heartbeat is steady and his lungs seem strong enough. However, I fear that both his legs are broken and will take some time to heal."

"What Hosea said is true," Deborah sighed. "We should have repented of our evil ways. There has been so much wickedness around us that we feared Hosea would be murdered while on the judgment seat, as was his brother Lachoneus."

Jael could no longer bear to listen. Chanting verses from her childhood, she rubbed warmth into the children's limbs in rhythm to her rhymes.

"Milk of goats and butter of kine,
Bread of wheat and grapes of the vine,
Fat of lambs and honey of bees,
I shall feed the child on my knees."

"Fat of lambs?"asked a boy at her side. "We have three new lambs in our shed, and they are all scrawny."

Jael grinned, amazed to find anything to smile about in the dark vapors. "I suppose newborn lambs are rather scrawny."

"So are newborn babies," said Dinah.

"Yes." Jael recalled the many babies she had seen at birth.

"Little Jacob was nothing but bones for months after he was born," added Dinah.

"I fat now," said the smallest child in Jael's lap. He took her hand and patted it against his round belly.

She hugged him more tightly and went on with her rhymes. After a time, the verses turned to songs, which seemed to calm her own dark thoughts and soothe the children's shivering.

"Jael, your songs are lovely," Deborah said. "I believe they have eased Hosea's pain."

Moments later, Mathoni called to her. "Jael, we shall need your help while we roll this pillar off Hosea. But leave the children where they are for now."

"Dinah, you watch the little ones." Jael handed the two smallest children to their sister. Then she crept slowly toward Mathoni's voice. "Where do you want me?"

"This way," he said. "Keep coming toward my voice. Good. Now, step over the pillar."

Jael's hands combed the dark area before her and contacted the rough stone. The pillar was nearly a cubit in diameter. No wonder Hosea's family could not move it. As she stepped over,

Mathoni's hand brushed her skirts.

"There you are!" he said, then laughed unexpectedly. "Now is when we could use that timber you thought you stumbled over."

"Oh, please, Mathoni!" Anger rose in her voice. "Why must you continue to laugh at me?"

"And why must you take life so seriously?"

"The whole world has crumbled around us, and you tell me not to take life seriously?"

Mathoni blew out a lungful of air. "What I need you to do is pull Hosea free, while Deborah and I hold up the pillar with the heavy cording I have tied around it." He took Jael's hands, anchored them on Hosea's wrists, then moved away. "Ready?" Mathoni grunted. "Now, Jael! Pull!"

She tugged with all her might. A full grown man! How could she possibly budge him? "Please, help me, Lord," she prayed. Her back arched, her knees stiffened, her shoulders wrenched. Finally the strength came. She pulled Hosea back a few cubits, then she breathed a "Thank you" and knelt beside him. "I hope I did not cause you more pain."

"No," came a feeble response.

Anxious moments passed as Mathoni tried to straighten the misshaped legs. Jael wished for a light so she might watch him use the skills he had learned from his father. Already he had gathered pieces of a broken table to use for splints. Jael held the wood in place while he wrapped Hosea's legs with strips of cloth.

"Thank you, Mathoni," Deborah sighed. "Surely you have saved the life of my husband."

Mathoni reached over and helped Jael to her feet. "I shall return in a few days to see if there is anything further I can do. Or I shall ask my father to come."

"Your parents made it through the earthquake?"

"I am not sure." Mathoni's voice tensed. "I was not at home

when the turmoil began. I am on my way there now. It is my hope that my family is all right."

"Your mother, Rebekah, has been a dear friend for many years. She must be proud to have a son such as you."

"And I am blessed to have her for my mother."

"Thank you, Mathoni," Hosea said softly. "You have helped us beyond measure."

"And you have also helped me."

"What do you mean?" asked Deborah.

"Because of you, I know what street we are on and where we must go to reach my house. Before now, I was uncertain."

Jael shuddered and clutched her arms across her chest. All this time, she had trusted Mathoni to lead her safely through the darkness, and he had been just as lost as she!

FOUR

After they left Hosea's courtyard, Jael stopped abruptly and put her hands on her hips. "You lied to me!"

"I did not." Mathoni tried to push her forward again. "I said I knew where my house was and that I had lived there all my life. I did not say I knew how to find it. Hah! That would have been a lie!"

Jael's back became rigid. She longed to wrench his arm off her waist. "Why are you doing this?"

"You act as if I am torturing you."

"Teasing me." She sounded more childish than she planned.

"Oh?"

Jael sensed he was trying not to laugh out loud. She shook herself free from his grasp.

"Do you want to go on from here alone?" he asked.

She stood silently, pondering a response. Then the ground began to quiver. She tried to remain on her feet, while a few voices screeched in terror. A nearby wall crashed to the ground. Dust poured into the darkness. Jael choked. She pulled the shawl across her face. Soon the earth stilled.

Mathoni tapped his stick impatiently. "How long do you plan to stand here? I thought you were eager to get home."

"I am ready to go," she said through the shawl.

"Shall I hold onto you, or would you prefer to hold onto me for a while?"

She laid the shawl back on her shoulders. "Just do what you have been doing." Once again, his arm found her waist and he slowly tapped his stick up the hill. As the incline steepened, Jael breathed raggedly, struggling over fissures and stones she could not see. The darkness seemed to taunt her like a vile beast. Her damp skirts weighed down her aching body. She shivered with each wailing voice that rose around them. How she longed to cover her ears!

"We have reached the highway!" Mathoni exclaimed as if he had struck gold. "Now we only must cross it and . . ."

"No!" Jael planted her feet and refused to move. "We cannot cross it. There is a deep crevice down the middle."

"There is?" Mathoni sounded unconvinced.

"I saw the highway sever with my own eyes." Her voice was thick with emotion.

"Perhaps you had better hold onto me." Mathoni forced her to wrap her arms around his waist. As he pulled her close, his warm cloak fell across her back and tempered the chill from her damp clothing. Then the stick tapped, and he nudged her forward. Seconds later they stopped. Mathoni leaned over to probe with the stick. "There truly is a crevice. We shall have to jump across it."

Jael shook her head, bobbing against his shoulder. Her anxious hands clutched the sash at his waist.

"Though the chasm is deep—more than the length of my stick—it is not very wide. Less than two cubits."

"You lied to me before."

"I did not lie to you. Believe me, my house is just a ways up this hill. I have brought you this far in safety. Will you please trust me for a few more minutes?"

Jael swallowed hard. "All right. I shall do as you say."

"Good." He pried her tense hands from his sash. "After I get across, I shall reach back with the stick. You take it and jump, while I pull you over."

Mathoni let go of her waist. With a grunt, he heaved himself over. "That was easy! And I am not lying. Now, Jael, take the stick." She heard it swish in her direction. Her trembling hands caught hold. "Count to three, then jump."

Jael took in a gulp of air and bent her knees. "One, two, three." She took a leap as the stick jerked, and she sailed through the air. Landing on solid ground, she did not hesitate to grasp hold of Mathoni. Again she welcomed the warmth of his cloak on her back.

As they followed the hilly pathway, each small step became harder for her tired legs. The black vapor stung her throat and lungs. Her arm that had combed the darkness for obstacles finally dropped to her side, and she relied more heavily on Mathoni to sustain her gradual forward motion.

After a time, he sniffed the air and said, "There have been many fires here. It is an older part of town, with more homes built of timbers. I hope my house is not one that was burned."

Jael's throat constricted. And what of her own house? Would she ever see Mother again? Her hand clenched Mathoni's sash so fiercely that the blood drained, and her fingers tingled.

Then from the darkness came a woman's weeping. "Oh, Lord, please send someone to help us."

Mathoni quit walking.

"Dear Father, deliver us from this darkness," prayed the woman, "that someone may find us and ease our pain."

"I hear you," Mathoni called through the thick vapor. "I am Mathoni, son of Zedekiah. Who is it that cries for help?"

"Mary, wife of Abram. We have suffered burns from the fires."

Mathoni patted Jael's side. "I know them well. They are elderly. I must help them."

Jael took in a weary breath but did not speak.

"My house is not far from here. I could take you there first and come back."

"No. Go see what you can do while I rest here a moment." Jael listened to the thud of his stick as he moved away. "Let me know if you need my help."

Groping for a place to sit, she found a boulder nearby in

what might have been a rock garden. She settled upon it and propped her head in her hands. A breeze stirred the smoky vapors, made her cough, and whipped tall stalks of grass against her legs. She reached down to brush the grass aside and got a handful of daisies, broken and drooping after the storm. Snapping off a few stems, she braided the stalks into a circle to make a crown as she had often done for festivals. Mother had taught her to make crowns and other ornaments for her hair. The smell of the daisies made her recall that Seth, as a toddler, had asked her to make an "ordinance" for his hair.

Jael's mouth curved into a slight smile. How she longed to be reunited with both Mother and Seth! Alone in the darkness, there was little else than that hope to cling to.

Footsteps crunched nearby. "Jael? Where are you?"

"Here, Mathoni. Are you finished already?"

"Yes. Their burns were minor, though quite painful for such elderly people. I filled a basin with cool water from their rain barrel so they could immerse the burned areas and ease the pain. Later, while you rest, I shall bring them back a salve of olive oil mixed with tree resin, which will keep the skin soft and free of infection." Mathoni reached down and found her shoulder. "Come. You are weary and cold."

Jael got to her feet and leaned against him as he urged her inch by inch up the hill. Before long, he turned left. "If I am not mistaken, my house should be about here." Together they stepped up a small embankment of earth. The stick tapped, stopped, tapped again. "Thank goodness!" he exclaimed. "The house is still standing." They felt their way along the weathered wooden wall until he said, "I found the door," yet he did not immediately lead her inside.

"Is something amiss? Do you fear going in?"

"I am taking off my sandals. They are covered with mud."

"So are mine." Jael leaned down, untied the leather straps, and slipped her feet out. Though she remembered that her clothes were also muddy, she was not about to leave them on the doorstep.

"Come," he said simply and opened the door. "Mother? Father? It is I, Mathoni. Are you all right?"

There came a stirring of bedstraw from a far corner, then an elderly woman's voice. "Mathoni? You are alive?" Footsteps shuffled in their direction. "Come, my son. Come to me."

Mathoni moved toward his mother's voice. Jael heard their muffled embrace, then the rhythm of their hushed voices.

"Where is Father?"

"Tending to the injured, wherever he can find them."

"I should be with him."

"Your brother went to help."

"Then Mathonihah, too, is all right?"

"He is well enough." The woman sighed. "I only wish I had word of your sister Martha and her young family."

"I shall go to them and bring you word."

"It is long way to the river."

"Yes, Mother. But I must journey that direction to escort Jonas' cousin Jael home to care for her mother."

"Little Jael?"

"Little? Hah! She is taller than you, Mother, and just as much a woman."

Jael flinched, and blood rushed to her cheeks. "I came in with Mathoni," she said rather awkwardly.

"Come closer, dear," spoke Rebekah's soft voice. Jael groped her way forward and found the woman's wrinkled hand. Then Rebekah drew her into a gentle embrace. Though her shoulders were bent with age, her voice was strong. "Jael, your clothing is wet. Let me find you something dry to wear." She led Jael slowly toward one corner of the room. "Is your Uncle Nephi all right? After the storm and earthquakes, people will need the blessings of a high priest."

"He was injured slightly by a beam that fell," Mathoni

answered for Jael. "But he shall mend soon enough."

"And the other members of Nephi's family?"

"They have survived the earthquakes," said Jael, keeping the hope that Mother had also survived. She heard the slight rustle of fabric then felt Rebekah's frail hands hold a dress to her shoulders.

"This should do nicely. It used to belong to Mathoni's sister, Martha." She paused to rummage for other items in the trunk. "Here are some dry wrappings for underneath. Take off your wet skirts, and I shall help you put these on."

Jael could not make herself move. Mathoni had joked about her womanly figure, and now she had to undress in the same room with him?

"Hurry," Rebekah prodded. "You are trembling with cold."

"But . . ." Jael could not voice her concern. It made no sense, considering the dark vapor that obscured the room.

"I will not look," Mathoni teased, once again guessing her thoughts. "I shall turn my back. But there is little I have not seen in my apprenticeship with Father, though we have treated fewer women than men."

Anger stiffened Jael from head to foot. How dare he make a mockery of her! She untied the band at her waist, unwrapped the layers of skirting, then slipped out of her blouse. Unwinding the strips of cloth from her loins, she replaced them with the dry bands Rebekah offered. Finally she lifted the dress over her head. Though it hung loosely around her shoulders and hips, the spun cloth felt warm against her chilled flesh.

Rebekah helped Jael tie the sash, then reached out with one more item. "Take my shawl."

"I cannot—" Jael started to protest.

"I shall not need it. I do not plan to go out in the darkness. It is an old woman's shawl—long and of thick wool. It will provide warm protection for your journey."

"Mother, we shall also need food for our journey," said

Mathoni from across the room.

"Surely you do not intend to leave right away?"

"Soon," Mathoni answered. "It took us perhaps two hours to get this small distance from Nephi's. It may take two days to make it to the river, depending upon the amount of destruction. But we shall rest a while and eat a meal before we leave."

"Why not abide here for the night?" asked Rebekah.

"For the night?" Mathoni sounded impatient. "This darkness is prophesied to last for three days. How shall we know when the night ends and the morning begins?"

FIVE

A two-day journey? wondered Jael with a quiver of fear. How could that be when it usually took but two hours to get home?

"Come, dear, you are shivering." Rebekah led her to the bed and pulled back the blankets. Exhausted, Jael let herself sink into the cloth-covered straw. Nestling in nearby, Rebekah reached over and ran her fingers through Jael's hair, just like Mother used to do. The pleasant sensation soon soothed her into slumber.

Jael dreamed in peace until a door banged open. She raised her eyelids, yet saw nothing. She closed her eyes, hoping to fade back into sleep. Beside her, Rebekah breathed steadily. But across the room, voices bantered, keeping Jael awake.

"How could you get here so quickly?" asked Mathoni.

"How could I not?" came Jonas' firm reply. "It is but a short distance from my house to yours."

"Hah! With the darkness, the heaps of debris from the quake, the crumbling streets and severed highway? And you would have me believe you made it here in a matter of minutes?"

"I let the Spirit lead me. That is the only sure guide through such stubborn mists of darkness."

"Do I detect a bit of pride, Jonas?"

"Forgive me if it sounds like pride, rather than trust in the Lord," Jonas said calmly. "Father asked me to go with you and Jael to check on Aunt Esther as well as on Uncle Timothy and his family. I believe the best way to travel is with the Spirit leading us."

"I have prepared only enough food for me and Jael."

"I have my own supplies." Jonas rustled his satchel, then added with mirth, "And the Spirit will not ask for sustenance."

Jael felt a smile creep upon her face. Sleep had been good for her. She wondered how long she had slept and how long since the terrible upheavals began. Then she bolted upright, jarring Rebekah awake. "Forgive me. I did not mean to startle you. I am worried about Mother. I must hurry home."

"Jonas and I are ready anytime," Mathoni announced. "Though I fear I have depleted my family's food supply."

"Not to worry, dear," Rebekah said as she arose from the bed. "We have stored much grain, and there is more dried meat in the smokehouse. Nephi was wise in telling us to make provisions against this prophesied day of destruction. Would that more people had listened to his warning voice." She shuffled toward the sound of Mathoni's voice. "Did you find the raisins?"

"Yes, and I have just finished eating my fill. I have also prepared a meal to give Jael strength before we leave."

Jael pried herself from the warmth of the straw bed and straightened Rebekah's shawl at her shoulders. Crossing the room toward the voices, she bumped against a chair.

"Jael, is that you?" Jonas reached out to grasp her wrist. "Come sit beside me." He guided her toward an empty chair at the table.

"Here," said Mathoni, shoving a plate toward her. "I have soaked some yams to soften them for you, and there are raisins and some of Mother's bread."

"Thank you." Her hands found the plate, and she ate eagerly, not realizing how hungry she had been. The raisins were plump and sweet, and she relished each one on her tongue.

"Here are two senines of gold for your journey," said Rebekah, and Jael heard the clink of coins.

"What good will money do in this darkness?"

"You may find need," Rebekah said softly. "I would feel relieved if you also took your father's sword. It is in its sheath beside the hearth."

While savoring the last bite of bread, Jael heard Mathoni's footsteps move toward the hearth, then he crossed behind her to the door. After a moment he came to her side. "Here are your sandals. I cleaned off the mud. May I help you put them on?"

"No, I . . ." she started to protest, then remembered the near proximity of Rebekah, who would be pleased at her son's gallant offer. "Thank you, Mathoni." She felt his warm hand on her ankle. His touch was more tender than she expected. A slight quiver rose up her leg. She dismissed the sensation and slipped her foot into the second sandal. "Thank you," she said again, feeling a bit breathless.

"Ready to go?" Jonas asked, unaware of what Mathoni's touch had done to his cousin.

Jael remained silent, thoughtful, while Mathoni asked his mother for a flask of wine. With all the destruction, he said the water might be contaminated with debris.

"There is one flask, hanging beside the door. Your father and brother took the medicinal wine with them."

"I have a bit of wine with me," said Jonas.

Jael stood up. "Is there something I could carry?"

"Hah!" Mathoni's voice made her flinch.

"Jael is young and strong," Rebekah said firmly. "I have seen her hauling both laundry and young children at the river."

"Yes," Jael said. "I do washing and tend children for women who are sick or near childbirth."

"And you assist your mother as a midwife," said Rebekah.

"The frailer she becomes, the more I must assist her."

"All too soon you shall be old enough to bear your own sons and daughters."

Mathoni chuckled at their women's talk. Jael felt redness on her cheeks.

Rebekah quieted him by saying, "To be a mother in Israel is a sacred and noble calling. Raising righteous children requires more heroism than any soldier could hope to sustain."

"Yes, Mother. And speaking of soldiers, we may need some bedding to sleep in, as on the battlefield."

"Yours and your father's bedrolls are here, ready to go." She moved toward a far corner. "But we only have the two."

"I brought my own blanket for warmth against the vapors of darkness," Jonas said.

"Is the purpose of this darkness to bring us to remembrance of the Lord?" Rebekah asked.

Jonas answered, "It was the prophet Abinadi who said we are a stiff-necked people, quick to do iniquity and slow to remember the Lord our God."

Rebekah shuffled back to the table. "Here are the bedrolls."

"I shall carry one," said Jael.

Rebekah reached for Jael's hands. "Be careful, dear."

She felt a knot of worry in her stomach and pressed the bedroll against it.

"We shall look after Jael," said Mathoni.

"I shall not require looking after," she insisted.

"I held you on your feet most of the way here."

"I am stronger now that I have slept!" Her burst of defiance melted the slight affection she had felt towards Mathoni. Now that Jonas had joined them, she planned to stay at his side, and his side only, during her journey home.

"Oh, Mother, I nearly forgot. When Father returns, would you ask him to check on the chief judge, Hosea? He was wounded by a fallen pillar. Father should make sure I set the bones correctly so they will heal."

"Yes, I shall tell him," said Rebekah. "What a blessing that Hosea was not killed by the pillar."

"Hosea lives on," said Jonas, "just as the words of the

prophet Hosea live on in the brass plates."

"You and those brass plates!" moaned Mathoni. "Come, it is time to leave."

"We must first offer a prayer to invoke the Spirit to guide us," said Jonas.

Jael bowed her head and calmly listened to her cousin's words. Yet she remained uneasy as she said goodbye to Rebekah and went out the door. Taking Jonas' hand, she let him lead her up the hill. With her other hand she gripped the cording tied around the bedroll.

Mathoni walked a short ways ahead, rapping his stick along the unpredictable terrain. Their progress was slow as they ascended the hill and skirted the hazards. Jael locked her concerns for Mother in the back of her mind, for there was enough to worry about just walking. She often stumbled over upturned stones or debris. And she could not get used to the bitter taste of the damp, smoky vapors.

With the little ground they seemed to cover, the more she wondered if they could make it to her home. "How shall we find our way to the river if we cannot follow the highway?"

Mathoni hastened to speak. "We will continue up this hill, past the temple, to the northern gates of the city wall. Then we shall continue north through the vineyards until we reach the stream, which will take us eastward to the river."

Jael squeezed her cousin's hand. "Do you think that is the best way to go?"

"I have tried to listen to the Spirit," Jonas said meekly.

"How can you hear anything with the endless howling of people on every side?"

"The Spirit is not heard with the ears, but with the heart."

"And what does your heart say?"

"To go out the northern gates, find the stream, follow it to the river, then go upriver to your house."

"Hah!" Mathoni exclaimed. "Precisely what I thought!"

"The Spirit has given us both the same message," said Jonas in a humble tone.

His mild words were comforting to Jael's heavy heart. She knew she could trust Jonas as much as she did Uncle Nephi. But as for Mathoni, she could not be so certain—partly because of his teasing nature—though she might trust him more if she could read the expression on his face. Staring straight ahead, she tried to picture him as he tapped his way along. What came to mind was the sight of him beside Uncle Nephi's hearth, fanning the flames into a brighter blaze. Strangely for a moment, Jael felt a glow of warmth. Then she recalled the protection Mathoni had offered her on the way to his house. Perhaps she should trust him more.

"Stay to your right," his voice suddenly boomed.

Jael gripped her cousin's hand more securely.

"What is it?" Jonas asked.

"Just stay to your right!" Mathoni said in a hostile tone.

Jonas asked no further questions but steered Jael to the right. After a few minutes the hill leveled out, and there seemed to be less clutter. Jael breathed a sigh of relief.

"There is not such a smoky smell in this part of town," Jonas said. "I believe the temple is close by. Surely the Lord has spared His temple from destruction."

"Hail!" a deep voice called through the darkness.

"Hail!" Jonas and Mathoni shouted in unison.

"Are you able men?" the voice called again. "Will you help us carry some wounded people to shelter?"

"Certainly!" called Mathoni, rapping his stick toward the voices.

"Will you be all right here alone?" asked Jonas, ready to release Jael. When she did not respond, he urged her to take a few steps to her left. "We are near the temple courtyard. You should be safe there."

Jael groped her way alongside Jonas until her fingertips

scraped a stone wall.

"Here we are," he said. "Wait by the courtyard wall, and I shall soon come back to get you."

She listened to his footsteps as he worked his way to the men who were exchanging words with Mathoni. Then she lay her arms atop the waist-high wall and gazed toward where she thought the temple stood. If only she might see just one oil lamp burning! As a small child, she had learned to look to the temple for peace in times of sorrow. Now it had vanished from view. A pang shuddered through her.

She tried to envision the temple and its courtyards, lit with candelabra for the Feast of Tabernacles. During those annual festivities, their family would set up a booth in the courtyard beside other relatives' booths for seven joyous days of feasting, dancing, singing, and religious rites. Last year, she had frolicked with Uncle Timothy's daughters, flirting with male cousins and their friends. That had resulted in a double wedding for Uncle Timothy's middle daughters. Her heart warmed at the memory of their marriage celebrations. As the next oldest young woman, Jael had been asked how soon her own betrothal might take place.

Her mood was brighter when Jonas and Mathoni returned to continue their tedious journey. After a while, the hill began to descend. Again her feet confronted an uneven pavement and rubble strewn by the quake. She tucked the bedroll cording over her shoulder so her hand was free to push limbs and other obstacles aside. Then a low moan caught her attention, quite unlike the steady lamenting of people. "What is that mournful sound?" she asked.

"And that repulsive smell?" added Jonas.

"A very unhealthy cow," replied Mathoni. "Watch your step now, Jael, so you will not trip over its timber-like legs."

Her hand shot out, wanting to push Mathoni aside for teasing her. But he was out of reach. She balled her hand into a fist.

Why did he have to be so insensitive? As a physician he ought to show more compassion to others. Forgetting to shield herself, Jael let something whip her forehead. She clenched her teeth against the slashing and continued forward, once again sweeping her hand through the thick vapor.

Then the ground began to shake and tilt. Jael grabbed onto Jonas' cloak, and he put an arm across her shoulders. Nearby buildings crackled with the upheaval, while she huddled against her cousin. As the quaking ceased, she found herself contrasting Jonas' slighter build to Mathoni's breadth. Her heart fluttered. She quickly dismissed the odd sensation and asked, "Shall we never be finished with earthquakes?"

"Perhaps they will go on for days like the vapors of darkness." Once again, Jonas took her hand, and they fumbled their way forward.

The tremor had magnified the eerie howlings on every side. Jael longed to press her hands to her ears but had to keep combing the dark fog. "Jonas, did Samuel the Lamanite say what is to happen when the three days of darkness are over?"

"Not in great detail, though he did deliver many profound prophecies."

"Will you tell me more about him?"

"Must you?" Mathoni groaned as he slowly led them along.

"It is better to listen to Jonas' words than to people wailing all around us." She stubbed her toe against a jagged stone and whimpered in pain.

"See?" said Mathoni. "You cannot walk and talk at the same time."

"Then Jonas shall do the talking." She bit her lip against the pain in her toe and continued groping her way forward. "How long ago did Samuel prophesy?"

"When my father was about my age. At that time, our Grandfather Nephi and his brother Lehi were also prophets in the land. Yet the people hardened their hearts and refused to listen to any of the prophets. They drove Samuel from the city several times. Finally, he stood high upon the city wall to raise his voice, while the people shot arrows and threw stones at him. But the Lord preserved him to deliver his message." Jonas let go of her hand. "Just a minute, I have a pebble in my sandal."

Jael heard him bend down and remove the pebble. "Did other prophets see our day and tell of what would happen when the darkness ended?"

"Yes." Jonas urged her slowly onward.

"Will you tell us of them?"

Again Mathoni groaned.

Jonas ignored his friend's murmuring. "Do you understand why this destruction and darkness have occurred?"

"Yes, I think so. Because Jesus Christ has died."

"And the earth is mourning the death of its Creator." Jonas paused to help Jael across a rough piece of ground. "Our fore-father Nephi prophesied of the thunder and lightning and earthquakes at the time of Christ's death. Following the destruction, Nephi said the Lord would appear in this land. Alma and Amulek also taught that after Christ's atonement and resurrection, He would visit the people here."

A twig lashed Jael's ankle and snagged on the hem of her dress. She stopped to pull it free. "Wait, Mathoni!"

He impatiently pounded his stick against the ground. "Do you realize that all your talk has slowed our pace?"

"I believe it is the darkness which hinders our pace," Jonas said to him.

"I am the slow one," said Jael. "Forgive me." For a time she moved in silence, concentrating on each placing of her feet. She was not acquainted with the northern portion of the city. Her usual route home was through the east gates, closest to Uncle Nephi's. Once she had traveled out the west gates to Zarahemla, but the north and south gates were unfamiliar. Tugging on Jonas' hand, she asked, "Where do the northern gates lead?"

"Nowhere," he answered.

"To the land of Desolation," explained Mathoni. "Though there are some verdant hills between here and there. We used to go to those hills to practice with our bows and arrows so we could become mighty soldiers."

"We were never very good," said Jonas.

"Mathonihah seemed to have a natural talent for it, though," mused Mathoni.

Jael carefully stepped over some fallen timbers. "I thought your brother was crippled. How could he go into the hills?"

"Mathoni carried him on his back for many years," said Jonas.

Jael nodded. She had often seen Mathoni as a boy with his brother on his back. But she thought it was merely part of a game they played together. "Was Mathonihah crippled from birth?"

"Yes. One of his feet was badly deformed."

Jonas gripped Jael's elbow and helped her through some clutter. "When Mathonihah grew too big to be carried, Mathoni made him a crutch and taught him how to use it."

Jael studied the darkness where she thought Mathoni was walking. Perhaps he was more compassionate than she thought.

"Mathonihah would have made a fine soldier," he said, rapping his stick.

"It is good he was not one of the wicked men who tried to shoot arrows at Samuel the Lamanite," said Jonas. "His arrows would have found their mark."

"Watch out for this low branch," Mathoni suddenly warned. "It whacked me a good one on the shoulder."

"I have it," said Jonas. "Duck underneath, Jael."

A plaintive cry for help shattered the dark air.

"No!" Mathoni firmly spoke. "I refuse to listen anymore."

SIX

"Someone is in need again," said Jael.

"I know." Mathoni said in a harsh tone. "I am not deaf."

Jael's brow wrinkled. "Are you upset about something?"

"We shall never make it to the aid of your mother if we stop to help everyone who calls to us from the darkness."

Jael shook her head. She sensed there was more to it than that, but rather than pursue it, she asked Jonas what he thought.

"I believe we should keep going, though it is difficult to ignore those who cry for help."

"It is difficult," Mathoni said with a softening in his voice. "But I truly feel there are greater needs awaiting us."

Jael sighed and followed him forward. The repeated cries for help hung stiffly in the black vapor. She hoped Mother was not also pleading for help. Crushing the bedroll against the prick of sadness in her chest, she stumbled along behind Mathoni. Rocks stabbed repeatedly at her toes. It was a blessing to not be able to see the torn and painful flesh.

"Here it is!" Mathoni exclaimed, jarring Jael's mind from her concerns. "The wall that circles the city."

"It has not fallen in the earthquakes?" asked Jonas.

"This portion still remains. And we should soon reach the northern gates."

Jael gradually felt her way along the high stone wall. It seemed intact, though chunks of stone had chipped off here and there, and she occasionally tripped over them.

After a while Mathoni stopped. "Something is amiss. I cannot—oh, yes, now I understand. I believe the archway over the gates has fallen and part of the wall beside it. We shall have to climb over the pile of stones."

"I shall help you climb, Jael," Jonas offered.

"Hah! She shall need no help climbing—only going down the other side."

This time Mathoni was close enough that Jael shoved him for his teasing. He fell against the stones, which shifted with a grinding noise. "Oh, I am wounded!" he groaned. "Help me."

Jael bit her lip. She could not believe that her slight shove had caused him such grief. Then she heard a chuckle deep in his throat. "Oh, please, Mathoni!" she protested. "Why must you continue to laugh at me? Jonas, talk to him."

Jonas cleared his throat. "What would you have me say? He is merely making light of a tense situation, as he always does."

Jael heard stones crunching together.

"These stones are loose," Mathoni said, serious once again. "It would be best to climb over them one person at a time."

"How high is the pile?" Jonas asked.

"That has not been revealed to me," said Mathoni in a mocking tone. "I will let you know when I reach the other side."

While Mathoni scrambled up the pile, Jael tucked a strand of hair behind her ear and glanced toward Jonas but found it useless to try to see him through the murky blackness.

"The pile of stones is perhaps six cubits high," Mathoni finally called. "And it is much easier than the last pile you scaled, Jael. Stay to the left and you should be all right."

Jonas grasped her elbow to assist her. "Go slowly."

Determined not to slip, she took careful handholds and footholds. Her fingers and toes jabbed into the stones, chipping her nails, but she made it to the top, then turned to go downward feet first. Partway down, Mathoni grasped her ankle, startling Jael, but she kept moving. Finding her waist, he eased her to the ground, then called for Jonas to come over. Mathoni's hands remained firm and warm on her waist until Jonas stepped to the ground beside them.

Then Mathoni's stick tapped to the right. "I think it is this way to the stream."

"Yes," Jonas replied. "I believe you are right."

"Did the Spirit warn you of that pile of rocks?"

"Oh, please, Mathoni!" Jael exclaimed. "Must you continue to make a mockery of sacred things?"

"A mockery? I did not mean to . . ."

"I may not have as much knowledge as my cousin does in spiritual matters, but I do know that some things should remain hallowed." Jael reached for Jonas' hand. "And I am trying to learn more by asking questions."

"Forgive me." Mathoni sounded penitent. "Shall we go?"

"It has taken hours to simply reach the city gates," answered Jonas. "We yet have a long way to the river."

As Jael followed the sound of Mathoni's thudding stick, she noticed the air smelled fresher here, though there seemed to be no break in the black vapors. She hoped there would be less clutter to turn her ankles.

Then, as if he had heard her thoughts, Mathoni said, "I think I shall like it better here outside the city walls."

"Because there will be fewer piles of rubble?" she asked.

"No," he said, "fewer people crying out for help."

"Just because we cannot hear them," sighed Jael, "does not mean they have ceased their wailing."

"I know," said Mathoni. "How well I know."

Jael cocked her head to one side. There was something more to Mathoni's feelings than he would allow himself to say. But she sensed this was not a good time to delve into it. So she returned to her discussion with Jonas. "Do you truly believe that Jesus Christ will visit this land?"

"I believe the prophecies about His coming." Jonas' voice grew soft. "I hope I shall be worthy to meet Him, face to face."

"Meet the Son of God, face to face?"

"Yes, the Son of God, the Creator of heaven and earth, the Redeemer of the world. What a glorious day it shall be! The most blessed event of my life . . . of your life, also." Jonas drew in a long breath. "With all my heart I believe that Jesus Christ will visit the righteous who remain upon this land. Though no one is certain how soon the Lord will come after the light returns, Father believes He will appear at the temple. And I am to tell everyone I see to make the journey there."

"Think again," interrupted Mathoni. "You are not likely to see anyone or anything for days."

"You are right. It shall have to be people I meet and talk with but do not see." Jonas gently tugged Jael's hand to lead her around an obstacle. "Father said the temple is a good place to assemble and make an accounting of those in the land who remain alive. He would also have me tell Uncle Timothy to bring his family and others in their village to the temple."

"I am not certain I can travel all the way home and back to the temple in this darkness," said Jael.

"No," replied Jonas. "We shall not attempt to return to Bountiful until light is restored in the land."

The terrain at Jael's feet suddenly changed to spongy soil. She also noted a breeze in her hair that rustled nearby leaves.

"We have reached the vineyards," Mathoni announced. "From here it is uphill until we arrive at the stream. It should not be hard to walk a straight course between the rows of vines."

"Unless the earthquakes have thrown them to the ground," mused Jonas.

Mathoni slid the sword from its sheath. "I shall go ahead to clear the way."

"I remember climbing this hill as a boy," said Jonas, "to go fishing in the stream."

Mathoni's sword severed a vine. "I am not certain we caught

many fish."

"More often snakes and salamanders," said Jonas.

"Which I kept close at hand, in case my sister Martha became too arrogant."

The hill rose more sharply than Jael expected, and she hated the thick mud which oozed into her sandals. She tried to lift her skirt to keep it from dragging in the mud.

"Do you think I missed something in life, never having any sisters?" asked Jonas.

Jael nudged him with her elbow. "You did your share of teasing. Just ask Uncle Timothy's daughters."

"I had to keep a safe distance between me and them."

"Why?" Jael was cautious in stepping up the slanted ground.

"Aunt Judith was determined I take one of them to wife. It is a relief that three of the four are finally married."

"And the oldest has already given birth to a son. I assisted Mother in midwifing at her bedside a few months ago."

Up the muddy hill she struggled, with the filmy black air sucking in and out of her lungs. Though it was easier to follow the sound of Mathoni's slashing sword than his rapping stick, her footing was precarious. For every two steps, she seemed to slide backwards one. Again she anchored the bedroll strap on her shoulder so she might clutch the vines and pull herself along.

Jonas patiently helped her up the slippery slope. "Midwifing must be a joyful experience."

"More often than not. It has been a blessing to learn the skill from Mother. There is no better midwife in the land. I have watched her breathe life into babies who were too weak to fill their own lungs. I have seen her use both tonics and massage to save women from profound bleeding. She rarely loses a patient."

"I wish I could say the same," mumbled Mathoni.

"I am certain that your experiences on the battlefield are

much more harsh," she said to him.

"The cry of a newborn baby is nothing like the cry of a man mortally wounded." Mathoni fiercely whacked aside another vine. Jael hung her head and knew she could not bear to do what Mathoni did as a physician. As she listened to him slicing the vines, she wished he could pierce the dark vapor with his sword so they might see clearly where they were going. The thought made her want to smile, but climbing the hill and grasping vines took all her energy. No longer could she keep the borrowed dress from straggling in the mud. Nor could she maintain Mathoni's slow, but steady, pace. He would move ahead, then stop to poke his stick into the mud while waiting for Jael and Jonas.

"At least the earth is no longer quaking," said Jonas, trying to cheer her.

"Oh, please, do not say such a thing!" she cautioned. "Just your saying it might bring on a tremor."

"Hah! Jonas is not yet that much of a prophet."

Jonas struggled to help Jael over a tangled vine. "Few prophets have used their power to command the earth and make it obey. However, our grandfather Nephi did."

Jael yanked at the vine which had twisted around her ankle. Jonas finally tore it from the ground and tossed it aside. Jael let out a weary sigh. "Mathoni, I wish you would slow down. I cannot feel my way along as quickly as you."

He responded by whacking aside more vines.

Jonas took Jael's hand and urged her upward. "Mathoni is used to tramping these hills with soldiers when he serves as their physician."

"And he has an advantage over us with that stick to steer himself around obstacles," added Jael.

"Would you prefer to take the lead?" Mathoni asked. "I shall be glad to turn over both my stick and sword."

"Forgive me," Jael responded. "I should not murmur against

you. I know I would be lost without your leadership." A vine slapped her forehead then pulled against her hair. She reached up to loosen it, then continued onward. "Jonas, you mentioned Grandfather Nephi's power to command the earth."

"A man has power only if it is given him by the Lord."

"I remember some of the stories Mother told me about Grandfather." Jael came to a bank of mud, and her foot slipped. She grabbed her cousin's arm to keep from falling. Pain ringed her ankle. "Wait a moment, Jonas." She bent to rub the sore joint. How many long hours they had walked! Yet they had not reached the stream, and the river was still miles away. She shook her head. So far to travel, and so little strength left!

The pain in her ankle eased, and she forced her weary body forward, believing that each step brought her closer to Mother. More and more she loathed the black vapor that robbed her of sight and sat like a haunting burden on her shoulders. She tried to focus on more uplifting thoughts. "Jonas, tell me how Grandfather Nephi received such magnificent power from the Lord."

"Would that I had the plates so I might read it exactly, but I believe God said something like this to Grandfather: 'I will make thee mighty, even that all things shall be done according to thy word, for thou shalt not ask that which is contrary to my will. And thus ye shall have power among this people.'"

"Mother told me of when Grandfather created a famine to bring the people to remembrance of the Lord. And later when they repented of their evil ways, he called down rain from heaven. I used to love that story."

"It is not just a story," said Jonas. "It is history."

"It is not just a story," mimicked Mathoni. "It is history. Of course it is history! Everything is history: the brass plates, the plates of Nephi, all this destruction, even us!"

"What is wrong, Mathoni?" Jonas asked. "It is so unlike you to be disagreeable."

Mathoni did not reply immediately, but dug with his stick, making a sucking sound in and out of the mud. Then he said, "I am not certain. It is merely an uneasiness. Something perhaps that concerns . . ." He stopped without finishing his statement. They stood in a silence that seemed as thick as the vapors of darkness. Finally he spoke again. "Forgive me. Perhaps it is nothing. Come. We shall go on."

The momentary rest gave added strength to Jael's legs in grappling with the mushy terrain. Yet her heart seemed heavier, sharing Mathoni's uneasiness. She hoped he would say something further, but the only sound he made was in slicing the vines with his sword. Jael let Jonas lead her steadily up the hill. "Closer to Mother, closer to Mother," became the chant in her head that made her legs keep climbing.

After a long while, Mathoni stopped and turned to speak. "We have reached the brow of the hill and, I believe, the stream. There are willows growing here alongside it."

"Yes, I can hear the splash of water," said Jonas. "It sounds as if the stream is full after the storms."

"At least it has not overrun its banks," said Mathoni. "We are in enough mud as it is."

Jael tugged her skirt free from a stubborn vine. "I hope the river has not risen beyond its banks."

"You are quite devoted to that river," said Mathoni.

"What do you mean?"

Mathoni gave a long, hearty laugh and continued chuckling as he walked alongside the willows.

Jael twisted the sash at her waist. "Oh, please, Mathoni!"

"Perhaps you would share the humor with us?" suggested Jonas. "By now, we could all use a bit of mirth."

"It is just a memory."

The more Mathoni laughed, the more tense Jael became. She knew what amused him and hoped he would keep it to himself.

Then Jonas whimpered, "Jael, you are digging your finger-nails into my hand," which caused Mathoni to laugh harder. "Either stop laughing or share it with us, Mathoni. If you fail to do that, she may dig a hole right through my flesh."

Jael let go of Jonas' hand. And she quit walking. Jonas stopped beside her. "What is wrong? You are as tense as a coiled snake, and Mathoni is laughing as if he were insane."

"Jael does not like to be laughed at," said Mathoni. "But in this case, it is justified, for she brought it on herself."

"What are you talking about?" Jonas cautiously took her hand and began to pull her along.

"Shall I tell him?" asked Mathoni. Jael's jaw was too firmly set to answer, so he began his tale. "It was perhaps five years ago, after one of my first trips to the battlefield with my father. We were on our way back through the land Bountiful and stopped to let our horses drink from the river. Father, wearied from the long journey, sat down beside a tree and fell asleep. I was glad for a moment to leave the adult world behind me and look for a more youthful adventure."

"What did you find?" asked Jonas.

"You do not have to tell him," Jael said between her teeth.

"But I want to!" jeered Mathoni. "I walked a little ways upstream and found a herd of children playing in the river—not unusual for a hot summer day. Jael was there, watching after her brother and other young children. A few older boys had gathered enough scraps of cloth to make a long cord. They tied the cord on a high tree branch and took turns swinging out across the river. Then they would let go and drop into the water. It looked like just what I needed to refresh myself after weeks on the battlefield." Mathoni began to chuckle again.

"Did I miss something?" asked Jonas.

"No," insisted Jael.

"Yes, Jonas, you did," said Mathoni. "You would have enjoyed the swing across the river and plunge into the water as much as I did on that hot afternoon. But what followed was even better." Mathoni turned his head so his voice came directly toward Jael. "Perhaps you would like to finish the story? After all, I am only telling it from my viewpoint."

"I wish you had never begun it," she mumbled.

"It seems that the boys close to Jael's age had teased her about her fear of trying their swing. As I climbed from the river and sat on the bank to dry, she gave in to their taunting. She took hold of the cording and started swinging far out across the river. Then all of a sudden, she let go. But instead of dropping into the middle of the river, she let go near the bank and landed in a cubit-deep mudhole. When I walked over to help her out of the mud, she was so covered, she was unrecognizable. Even her mouth was filled with mud, which spewed out as she sputtered, 'Go away! Leave me alone!'" Mathoni let himself laugh freely. "As long as I live, I shall never forget how she looked sitting there in that mudhole."

Jonas did not laugh out loud, but Jael sensed the grin on his face. Her fingers continued to bore into the bedroll. She took firmer, defiant strides. Though nothing more was said, she heard an occasional chuckle from Mathoni.

After a while, he became silent, and Jael noted the quiet ripple from the stream. She took in a calming breath. It was a blessing to have such a steady lifeline of water, which not only offered peace but was there to guide her homeward. Perhaps Jonas would say that the Spirit also offered such peace and guidance. But right now she needed something more tangible to rely on, and the stream seemed to provide that.

For a brief time, Jael sensed renewed energy within her soul. Mathoni had slowed his gait, making it easier for her to grope her way forward without stumbling. Though the ground was mushy and uneven, fewer stones stabbed at her feet. Yet even at the slower pace, her energy declined, and she was glad when Mathoni came to a halt.

"What is it now?" Jonas asked.

"Nothing more than fatigue," Mathoni said. "Perhaps we should spread out our blankets and get some sleep."

"Here? In the mud?" Jael protested.

"Not right here," Mathoni answered. "If my memory serves me well, we are near a winery, where we could find shelter."

Before Jael or Jonas could respond, the ground began to tremble. Jael clutched onto a nearby willow as a shock wave rolled beneath her feet. Water sloshed from the stream, pouring over her sandals and splashing her skirt. She shivered from the chill.

When the quaking ceased, Jonas patted her shoulder. "Are you all right?"

"I am drenched."

"As am I," said Jonas.

"Now we shall have an additional cause for stopping at the winery," said Mathoni. "We can lay out our clothes to dry while sleeping in our bedrolls."

Jael braced her heels against the soil. She had no desire to undress again, wet clothing or not. "Could we not try once more to light a fire?"

"Hah!" Mathoni moved onward. "Where would we find dry wood after all the rain?"

"Where is your faith?" asked Jonas.

"I was not raised under a prophet's roof as you were," Mathoni snapped. "It is difficult, if not impossible, to learn faith on a battlefield. Faith makes no sense when I see my friends and neighbors bleeding from wounds inflicted by their brethren the Lamanites or the Gadianton robbers. And there is little use for faith when I have done all I can to save a man's life and still he dies."

SEVEN

Jonas pulled Jael to a halt. "Mathoni, you have passed the winery."

"How do you know?"

"I just do. Jael, wait here while I go check. I believe there is a bridge across the stream, where I noticed the sound of the small waterfall. The winery should be just beyond the bridge."

Glad to catch her breath, Jael stood and listened to Jonas' feet move away and Mathoni's footsteps nearing. Then all was quiet. She twisted the fringe of Rebekah's shawl and squinted in the direction where Jonas had disappeared. Finally she could no longer bear the silence. "Mathoni, if you did not learn faith on the battlefield, what did you learn?"

"Common sense, I suppose. How to pull an arrow from between a man's ribs, how to sew torn flesh together, how to splint a fractured thigh." He seemed thoughtful for a moment, then continued. "There are many things my father taught me: how to find the right roots and herbs to ease a man's pain, how to read the next day's weather from the evening sky, how to shoot a rabbit running through the brush and cook it for dinner." Mathoni dug his stick into the soil. "How to hold a dying friend in your arms and give him hope when there is no hope."

His final words sank deeply into Jael's heart. Perhaps Mathoni did feel compassion for others, but kept it deep inside.

"I was right!" Jonas called. "The winery is here, still in one piece. Come across the bridge."

"It looks as though you are stuck with me to get you across," said Mathoni. "Or would you rather go by yourself?"

"I shall hang onto you," she softly responded.

"As I recall, it is not a very wide bridge." Mathoni's brawny arm pulled Jael to his side. His thick cloak fell across her back, causing a mystifying throb in her heart. She tried to ignore the feeling and concentrate on matching his stride across the planking. Yet with each step she became more entranced with his warm body against hers. She breathed in the smell of his deerskin vest and let her fingers loop around the sash at his waist. When they reached the winery door, she was surprised at her reluctance to let him go. Yet Mathoni did not seem to share her enchantment. Without a word, he dropped his bundle on the stone floor and sat down beside it.

"There is a hearth with some dry wood," Jonas said from a far corner, "if you would still like to attempt a fire, Jael."

"It is up to you," she replied, still pondering the strange effect Mathoni had on her. For a moment she waited to see if he had further words to speak to her. But he remained silent, so she began to grope across the stone floor. "I am less concerned about a fire than finding a place to sit down and rest."

"Why not undo your bedroll and lie down?" suggested Jonas.

"But take off your wet clothes first," said Mathoni, stifling a yawn. "And remember, you have no need for concern, for we cannot see you in the darkness."

Jael's fingernails bored into the bedroll. Why did his teasing irritate her so? She ran her hands across the damp dress and wished it would dry without taking it off. Locating a short wall in the middle of the room, she sat down. The wall enclosed a large tiled vat that smelled somewhat moldy. "Is this where they make the wine?"

"I believe so," answered Jonas. "But I doubt there shall be much use for it this year."

"Why is that?"

"Did you fail to notice what the storm has done to the grape vines? They were nearly stripped clean of leaves and blossoms.

Unless they bloom again later this spring, there shall not be much of a harvest in the fall."

Jael's teeth began to chatter from her damp clothing. She reluctantly slipped the dress over her head, laid it on the wall to dry, and placed Rebekah's shawl beside it. At least the borrowed underwrappings remained dry, she thought, so she did not also have to remove them. Unfolding the bedroll, she wound it around her narrow frame and felt instantly warm within the layers of softly-quilted fabric.

Mathoni yawned noisily then said, "Jael, I have some dried venison in my satchel, if you would like something to gnaw on before you go to sleep."

"Yes, I would." Feeling her way across the floor, she reached Mathoni's corner near the door.

"There are also some dried currants." He filled her cupped hands.

"Thank you." Jael heard a clicking across the room. "What are you doing, Jonas?"

"Trying to start a fire." Jonas repeatedly struck rocks together. Jael looked in the direction of the sound. Not even the slightest spark lit the darkness.

"You mean you have to use flint like everyone else?" Mathoni taunted. "Faith alone does not work to start a fire?"

"Not tonight," said Jonas, patient with his friend's doubtful nature. "However, under the right circumstances it is possible to call down fire from heaven. The brass plates tell of Elijah performing such a miracle." Jonas plunked down his useless fire-stones. "I shall stretch out by the hearth anyway. Jael, would you like to come and sleep beside me?"

"Yes. That will be a fine place to spend the night."

"Night, day! What difference does it make?" moaned Mathoni. "It is not as though we shall wake up to see a sunrise."

Jael took her food and bedroll and crept toward Jonas. She heard Mathoni kick at his quilt to smooth it out. After a few minutes, he breathed steadily and deeply in slumber. "It is a gift to fall asleep that quickly," she sighed. "Though my body is weary, I am not certain I will be able to sleep. I am more likely to lie here and worry about Mother. Oh, Jonas, it seems like weeks since I was at her bedside!"

"And yet it cannot have been more than eight or ten hours since the vapors came upon us." Jonas yawned. "Would you like to talk for a while?"

"No. You go ahead and sleep. I shall doze off soon enough." Placing her hands behind her head, she stared up at the darkness that surrounded her like curdled milk, complete with a sour smell. In a corner she heard the scratching of a mouse. Or was it the slither of a snake? She listened harder. Only a mouse. She breathed a sigh of relief and slowly chewed on her dried food. The currants were tangy and brought moisture to her mouth, but the venison was stringy and coarse. She wished she had asked Mathoni for a drink from his flask before he went to sleep. The more she thought about it, the thirstier she became. Though still hungry, she laid the venison aside.

Thoughts of Mother came to mind. Jael pressed the quilted fabric against her eyes to hold back the sudden tears. A few weeks ago when spring weather arrived, she had gone to search the budding meadows for a new healing herb to ease Mother's violent cough, but it was still too early. Now the only chance was if someone more knowledgeable knew a cure. She would have to ask Mathoni when he awakened.

In the corner near the door, he began to snore softly. Jael pulled the quilt from her eyes and turned her head in his direction. She pondered his words about holding a dying friend to give him hope when there was no hope, and she realized he had also done that for her: provided hope when the world seemed hopelessly dark. More than that, he had set aside his own safety to help her travel home. A smile crept on her face. When she overlooked his teasing ways and doubting of spiritual matters, she discerned a pure core of goodness in Mathoni, which she would endeavor to see more of as time went by.

The stone floor grew harder and colder beneath her. She sat up, hugged her knees to her chest, then rocked back and forth as she softly intoned a psalm. "Sing unto the Lord, O ye saints of his, and give thanks at the remembrance of his holiness. For his anger endureth but a moment; in his favor is life: weeping may endure for a night, but joy cometh in the morning."

Jael shook her head. How could joy come if the morning did not? Her anxious hands picked at stray threads on the quilted bedroll. Then she spent a while scraping her feet clean of the caked mud which had collected during the day. Finally she wiggled free of the bedroll and groped toward the wall where she had left Rebekah's shawl. Wrapping it across her shoulders, she made her way to the door. Perhaps if she relieved herself, she could relax and sleep.

Jael silently moved outside and stayed beside the outer wall of the winery. As she came back in, the feeling of thirst once again overtook her. She decided to find Mathoni's flask. Her eager hand located it near his head. As she swallowed a generous mouthful, the wine caught in her throat, and she began to choke.

"Jael?" Mathoni's voice was sleepy. "Jael, is that you?"

"Yes," she coughed.

"I thought you were sleeping by Jonas." His voice got louder and closer. He must have sat up.

Finally her throat cleared. "I came to get a drink. Forgive me. I did not mean to awaken you."

"I understand." Mathoni reached out and contacted her bare knee. She jumped back. "Hah!" he chuckled. "Let me guess. You have been unable to sleep, so you came over for some company. Getting a drink was just an excuse."

Jael barely heard the last of his words as she crawled back across the winery. She again laid the shawl on the short wall, then she snatched up the bedroll and wound herself tightly inside. But she did not lie down. Nor did she sit. Her heart was beating like a trapped bird's with a predator stalking. She merely stood there waiting for the pulsing to cease.

"Jael, I am awake now," Mathoni said. "If you cannot sleep, we may as well talk."

"I would rather eat earthworms."

"Hah! If you are that hungry, perhaps you need a bit more venison to chew on?"

"No, thank you. That is what made me thirsty."

"Then should I bring you some currants?"

"Stay where you are!" Jael folded her arms across her chest, defying him to say anything more.

Jonas stirred and mumbled in his sleep.

"What did he say?" asked Mathoni.

Jael ignored the question.

"I suppose you would rather listen to Jonas talking in his sleep than speak with me." Mathoni began to sing a tune, which Jael recognized as an ancient soldiers' song. "Plead my cause, O Lord, with them that strive with me. Fight against them that fight against me. Take hold of sword and shield, and stand up for mine help. Draw out also the spear, and stop the way against them. Let them be as chaff before the wind."

Jael enjoyed his resonant voice, winding through the black vapor. She realized, that to sing such a song and to face what he did upon the battlefields, he must have more faith in the Lord than he was willing to admit.

"Are you sure you would not like to talk for a while?" he asked, when the song ended.

She continued to wait in silence.

"What happened? You cannot be asleep already." He had something in his mouth. He chewed for a moment, then spoke in a softer tone of voice. "Forgive me, Jael. I did not mean to startle you before, when I touched your knee. If you come over again, I promise to keep my hands to myself."

Jael was not sure how to respond. One moment she felt drawn to him, and the next she was angry at him. But one thing was certain: she was getting light-headed from standing so rigidly. Her choices were to lie down and try to sleep, or to talk with Mathoni to ease the dark, lonely hours. "All right. I shall come talk with you, but only for a short while." She found her way to his corner.

He patted the spot beside him. "Here, I have laid out my cloak for you to sit on."

She sat down and leaned her back against the wall. The stones chilled her, even through the thick quilt. And now that she was there, she could think of nothing to say to Mathoni.

"This has not been easy, has it?" he asked.

"What? Putting up with you all day?" Jael regretted her words as soon as she had spoken them.

"Hah!" Mathoni did not seem to mind her words. "What I meant was the difficulty in traveling through this darkness and destruction."

"I would not do it were it not for Mother." Jael drew up her knees and wrapped her arms around them. "Do you know of a cure for her lung disease that brings blood when she coughs?"

"Have you tried milk from the ephedra plant which grows in the desert?"

"Yes, we have used that in a tonic along with crushed vanilla bean. Also we have tried a poultice of bitter bark from quinine bushes."

"Those are the best cures I know for difficulties in breathing. But I am not certain they will heal the lesions that make her cough blood. I shall ask my father if he knows of a better cure." Mathoni was quiet for a moment then went on sounding like a physician. "I know you are concerned about your mother, but how are you feeling after your first day's journey? Do your feet hurt? And how about that knee you bumped earlier?"

She hung her head. "Does it matter?"

"It matters more than you think." Mathoni cleared his throat. "I have not been very considerate of your feelings today. I have forced you to grope through the darkness faster than you desired, and I have teased you too much. Forgive me, Jael. I have only been thinking of myself."

"In this darkness it is difficult to remember anyone else is there."

"For me it is just the opposite. I am painfully aware that I am not alone in this darkness."

Jael cocked her head to one side. "I do not understand."

"I would not expect you to." Mathoni readjusted the bedroll around him, then he became silent.

Jael listened to the mouse, rustling in a corner. She noticed Jonas' deep breathing. She heard Mathoni take a swig of wine from the flask, but still he said nothing. "I thought we were going to talk."

Mathoni put down the flask. "I have said too much already."

"Why are you so painfully aware that you are not alone?"

"I am an apprentice physician. For five years, all my training has been to help people when they are sick or wounded." He nudged the flask against her hand. "Would you like some?"

"No, thank you." She pushed the flask away. "I would like you to keep talking."

His voice was somber. "I know you have been troubled with people crying out through the darkness, as have I. But it is different for you. All you can do is feel empathy for them. I, on the other hand, have been trained with skills to help them. And yet, I am doing all I can to avoid using those skills."

"You helped several people in the city."

"Yes, until I could no longer bear their suffering cries. Then I chose to get as far away from people as I could by traveling alongside the stream."

"I thought the Spirit told you to go this way."

"What do I know about listening to the Spirit? That is what Jonas claimed, not I."

Jael reached over to touch his arm. "You are being too hard on yourself."

"I am hard on everyone."

"I noticed." Once again, Jael let herself smile. Truly, there was a core of goodness in him. He just preferred to keep it hidden.

Mathoni took her hand in his and gave it a squeeze, but she winced and drew it away. "You do not like me much, do you?"

"It has nothing to do with you. My hand is sore." She touched the palm and two of her fingers which were tender. "When I slid down that pile of debris, the timber I grabbed gave me splinters. I can feel them, poking from beneath the skin. I think they are beginning to fester."

"You and your timbers," said Mathoni, though this time he did not laugh at her. "Here, let me see."

"If you can see, it is a miracle."

"Hah! Let me feel, then. I shall be careful."

"You promised to keep your hands to yourself."

"This is different. Remember, I do have some medical training." Mathoni took her outstretched hand, and she guided his fingers to feel the tender spots. "I think I might be able to pull out a few of the splinters, if you would like."

"I wish you could see what you were doing."

"It will be more exciting this way. I only wish I had my satchel of medicines so I could put on a salve to soothe the festering."

"You have no medical supplies?"

"No. And that is also bothering me. I knew very well, after helping Hosea and others, that I should take my bundle of supplies when we stopped at my home. But I purposely left it."

"Why?"

"Too much pity, I suppose. I did not want to deal with it.

My heart grieves when I must attend to someone who is deathly ill or wounded severely. And there are always loved ones standing nearby, as with Hosea's family, so very hopeful that I will provide a miracle."

"Sometimes you do provide a miracle."

"Not nearly often enough." Mathoni touched the most prominent sore spot in her palm. "Should I give it a try?"

"Go ahead." She felt him take hold with his fingernails and gently tug until the splinter came out. "That feels better already. Try the one on my middle finger."

In no time Mathoni removed that splinter. "Any others?"

"Not until it is light and you can see what you are doing."

"I could wait a long while before the light returns. Until then, I can avoid seeing the faces of people who need my help."

"But you can still hear them."

"Not here by the stream." Mathoni held her hand between both of his. "There is something else bothering me. Remember the uneasiness I mentioned earlier?" He gently ran his fingers up and down the back of her hand and wrist. "It is hard for me to explain, but I have this curious feeling within me. I believe my medical knowledge will be needed in a tremendous way, even before we reach your mother's house. And for some reason, I think it has to do with my sister, Martha, and her family."

"Jonas would say the curious feeling within you is a prompting from the Spirit."

"Which makes it all the more foolish to leave my medical supplies at home."

Jael leaned her head against the stone wall. With Mathoni's hand stroking hers, sleepiness began to set in. She fought off the urge to yawn and asked, "If you do not enjoy being a physician, why did you not apprentice in another profession?"

"I do enjoy being a physician. What sorrows me is watching people suffer and die, while I can do nothing to help."

"No one likes to witness that. I, too, sorrow if a baby or

mother dies while I am assisting Mother." Her voice softened as pain twinged within her chest. "But the saddest bedside vigil I recall was when my father died."

Jael could not suppress the vivid memory: his body was crushed by a band of Gadianton robbers raiding the village. Father had tried to prevent their stealing a wagon from a widowed neighbor, and they trampled him with the team of horses. He was still alive when other neighbors brought him home and laid his broken body on the bed. Mother had begged him to hang on until Uncle Nephi could administer a blessing.

Jael pressed one hand against her eyelids that stung now as they had during that long night four years ago. Then suddenly she remembered that Mathoni had been there with Zedekiah, who was summoned to give aid. "Mathoni," she said in a whispered tone, "did you not sit on the floor by his bed all that night and the next day?"

He slipped an arm around Jael's shoulders. "When his heart quit beating, I asked my father if we could not get it started again. Never before had I felt such an intense desire to heal someone. And never before had I witnessed such devotion and faith in a family. You and your mother continued to talk with your father and hold him and nurse him, long after my father said he had done all he could."

"Mother believed his life could be restored through a priesthood blessing. But Uncle Nephi was several days' journey away preaching in Zarahemla, and by the time he returned to Bountiful, it was too late." Jael used the corner of her quilt to blot her tears. "Uncle Nephi has actually raised people from the dead, such as my Uncle Timothy. Did you know that?"

"Jonas mentioned it." Mathoni's fingers danced across her hand and arm. "But I am not convinced Timothy was dead."

"I would not know. I was not there." Jael sensed a deeper fatigue settling in. "I only know how hard it was to wait hopefully by Father's bedside and watch him die." Jael's eyelids felt limp and heavy. She leaned her head to one side. It came to rest on Mathoni's shoulder, and she surprised herself by letting it stay.

"Perhaps you understand why it is hard for me?"

"Yes." Jael let herself yawn.

"It sounds as if you are growing sleepy here beside me." Mathoni tipped his head so it rested lightly upon hers. "Perhaps you should close your eyes and sleep a while."

"My eyes are closed," she said.

"Oh," whispered Mathoni. "Are you comfortable?"

"Very."

Mathoni continued to stroke her arm, which soothed away the tension of the day. Jael took in a deep breath, released it, and within seconds she fell asleep.

EIGHT

"Jael, where are you?" Jonas called from across the winery.

Sleepily, she heard his voice but did not fully arouse until Mathoni jostled her. Then she was wide awake and in a hurry to get up. But Mathoni's firm hands held her where she was, with her head upon his shoulder. "No need to worry," he whispered. "Jonas cannot see us—uh, cannot see you."

"Jael?" Jonas called again.

"I am here, near the door."

"With Mathoni?"

"With Mathoni." She pried her weary head off his shoulder. "We were talking, and . . . I fell asleep."

"She speaks the truth," said Mathoni. "I put her to sleep with my chatter."

Jael rubbed her eyes and wished the darkness would vanish away. "How long did I sleep?"

"I cannot say, for I also slept. Are you rested enough to go on?"

"Yes, I think so. Perhaps after something more to eat." She felt a warm tingle as he gently pulled his arm from behind her head. Caught in the unexpected glow, she failed to hear Jonas approach and started at his words.

"I shall be right back," he said and stepped outside.

Mathoni rustled in his satchel, then he handed Jael some bread, cheese, and the flask of wine. "I shall join Jonas momentarily."

Jael heard him rise and leave. The side of her that had nestled against him was suddenly cold. She pulled the quilt more tightly across her shoulders and found herself longing for his return. Perhaps she could walk at his side today. With her decision to seek for goodness in Mathoni, she could now see little she did not like about him. But there was no way to be certain how he felt about her without seeing it in his eyes.

Mathoni and Jonas were talking merrily as they returned. "Would you believe there is a pink sunrise over the eastern hills?" Mathoni asked. Jael started to get up. "Hah! It is not true. I only said that to get you moving more quickly."

"I should have known you were teasing." Jael heard Jonas walk back to his spot near the hearth. She nibbled on her bread and cheese and listened to Mathoni fold up his bedroll. How odd it was that she had let herself fall asleep at his side, and with only the bedroll to protect her. The bread made a lump in her throat. She swallowed hard to make it go down.

"Give me your bedroll. I shall tie it up for you." Mathoni put his hand upon hers.

Jael dropped the cheese into her lap. A profound throb arose in her chest. She laid a hand there, hoping to conceal the sound from Mathoni.

"Your bedroll?" he prodded, patting her hand.

"I . . . I am cold."

"Yes, your hand is cold." Mathoni rubbed it gently. "We need to get you up and moving."

Jael wondered how she could feel chilled with her heart beating so wildly. Mathoni gave her hand a final squeeze before he let go. She chewed the last bite of cheese, then asked, "Did you get something to eat?"

"I shall in a moment, while you are dressing."

Jael's whole body went from cold to hot. If she failed to get up now, she may never move. She stood, stripped off the quilt, and handed it to Mathoni. Yet he made no teasing comment, as she had come to expect. He simply began to fold up the quilt. Jael found her way to the short wall and put on the dress, sash and shawl. Then she combed through her tangled hair with her fingers and walked back to Mathoni, who handed her the bedroll.

"Ready?" Jonas grabbed her by one elbow.

Disappointed that Mathoni would not be at her side, Jael followed Jonas out the door. Crossing the bridge, Mathoni stayed close behind, breathing warmly on the back of her neck. She longed to say something to him—anything! But her mind was as blank as the scene before her.

After the bridge, Mathoni went ahead with his stick, while Jonas led Jael around the overgrown bushes beside the stream.

"I thought the winery provided a good shelter while we slept," Jonas said.

"It also provided a good place for us to play during the winter seasons of our childhood," added Mathoni.

"Until we caused trouble there," added Jonas.

"That was a much later time, when my father sent me to obtain some medicinal wine." Mathoni paused, and Jael heard him whacking something with his sword. "It is no use," he said after a moment. "There is too much undergrowth here. We shall have to move to our right, but we shall keep listening for the sound of the stream as we walk. Come this way."

They followed Mathoni's direction, carefully skirting heaps of rocks and other unknown hazards. Jael waved her arms to protect her face from overhanging branches as well as thorny twigs which she guessed were wild roses. When the sound of water in the stream was barely audible, they turned again in an easterly course. Jael welcomed the slight downward sloping of the terrain, just enough to sustain the flow of water in the stream. The soil had dried considerably during the hours they rested, so her feet no longer slipped in the mud. Mathoni gradually led them forward, stopping often to warn of rocks or holes in the ground.

Jael's shoulders sagged as time passed. She tried not to think how much, for each minute gone was less time spent nursing

Mother back to health. She chided herself for leaving the bedside to go after Seth. If only she had sent him to Uncle Timothy, who lived closer, though there were no young sons at that house for Seth to play with during the days of midwifing. Jael knew a little sister would have been allowed to stay home and assist with the births. She smiled at the thought of having a sister. But never would she give up her brother, though sometimes he got into mischief, just as Mathoni and Jonas said they had at the winery.

"Jonas, why did the two of you get in trouble when you went after the medicinal wine?"

"It was not my errand, but Mathoni's. Let him tell you."

Mathoni gave a slight chuckle before he began. "The master of the vineyard was not to be found at the winery, though the tiled vat contained a considerable amount of the fermenting wine I had been sent to get. So we left to search the man's house and vineyards to find him." Mathoni chuckled again. "We found him at his brother's house nearly an hour later, and he went back with us to the winery. It seems we had forgotten to close the door, and a trio of goats from a neighbor's field had wandered inside the winery to greedily partake of the fermented wine." Mathoni gave a hearty laugh. "What a mess they had made in their drunken state!"

"You were not laughing when he made us clean up after them," Jonas reminded his friend.

"No. Remember how badly it smelled? Not only had the goats left urine and droppings everywhere, they also broke several jars of wine by butting or kicking the shelves on the walls where the jars were stored."

Jonas helped Jael over a rocky piece of ground. "I have not been back to that winery since then."

"Until yesterday," chuckled Mathoni.

Jael shook her head. "I am glad you told me that story after I slept there and not before."

Onward they walked with Mathoni's stick tapping and his voice cautioning them to stay to the right or left. Jael noticed an occasional scent of jasmine, drifting through the thick darkness. She flinched at the frequent prick of sticks against her sandaled feet. The borrowed dress often caught on shrubs or thorns, and they would pause to loosen the snags to prevent the cloth from tearing. As her legs grew more weary, her entire body began to droop with fatigue.

Finally Mathoni stopped and said, "Wait here by this fence." Jael braced herself against the crisscrossed timbers.

Jonas let go of her hand. "What is that awful smell?"

"Something that died," Mathoni huffed as he hoisted himself over the fence. "I shall let you know what I find."

Jael pressed the bedroll to her face, but it failed to diminish the rancid odor.

"This is incredible," Mathoni called after a moment. "An entire herd of dead cattle crammed against the fence. Why would they all die like this?" When next he spoke, his voice was low to the ground. "Now I understand. All their heads are pointed in the same direction. Perhaps they were frightened by the thunderbolts, broke into a deadly run, and became trapped by the fence and stream. Then, as others ran headlong into them, they simply trampled each other to death."

"Must we stand here forever?" asked Jael. "The odor sickens me."

"There is no way through." Mathoni came back over the fence and landed beside Jael, close enough that she could feel his warmth. She suddenly longed to have his arm across her shoulders to provide security to go on in the darkness. She reached out to touch him, but he had already moved away. "This way," he said. "Follow along the fence to your right until we find a place to pass through the field."

Jael sighed and began to grope her way along the crisscrossed timbers, careful to not get more splinters in her hand.

As the rancid odor diminished, Mathoni again hoisted himself over the fence, then called for them to join him.

Jael lifted her skirts. The scraggly timbers scratched her legs as she climbed over. She landed on Mathoni's foot. "Forgive me," she said softly.

He steadied her with an arm across her back. "My pleasure."

Jael smiled despite her fatigue. Jonas arrived beside them, and Mathoni turned to leave. His cloak fluttered behind him, brushing Jael's hand. Goose bumps rose up her arm. She rubbed the flesh smooth, then let Jonas take her hand.

"Mathoni, how far do you think we have come?" she asked as they moved onward.

"Not nearly far enough for the amount of time we have traveled."

"You seem to be taking it slower today," said Jonas.

"I did not want to tire Jael."

Her legs suddenly seemed lighter as she followed Mathoni, and she drifted into a dreamy state. But she soon discovered it was a mistake to not concentrate on walking. She stumbled. The ground thudded against her chest. She whimpered as pain spread through her torso. Jonas bent down and tried to help her up. "Wait," she said, trying to work through the pain. Her tense hands grasped at tufts of grass where she lay.

Mathoni came to her side. "Are you hurt?"

"I . . . I," the words would not form. She felt Mathoni's hands on her back, then her shoulders and neck. His touch was as a physician's: gentle, yet searching.

"Any pain here?" he asked.

"No," Jael breathed. "I am all right. Could you help me to stand?"

"Certainly." He grasped under her arms and pulled her upward. "At least the ground is not muddy as it was yesterday. May I carry your bedroll for a while?"

"It is no trouble." Jael wished he would offer to guide her, as he had the day before, with his arm at her waist.

"Perhaps you should hold onto my cloak and follow directly in my footsteps," he said.

"Would that I could see your footsteps." She reached out to grasp his cloak, then wished to herself that she could also see his face.

Jonas draped an arm across her shoulders. "I shall keep a tighter hold on you."

"Good." Mathoni's cloak tugged her forward. For a while, he seemed to take firm, deliberate steps. Jael, listening to his every move, tried to place her feet where his had been—tromping through clods of dirt and clumps of grass, then skirting boulders and bushes.

Jonas stayed patiently at her side. "The problem, Jael, is that you think of this darkness as a hardship."

"And you do not?"

"Three days of darkness are good for contemplation."

Jael's foot caught in a small hole. Jonas steadied her, and she gripped Mathoni's cloak more fiercely. "How can you contemplate anything? I can barely concentrate on walking, and even so, I stumble often." Jael stepped through a mass of tree roots. Though her knees ached, the cloak in her hand steadily pulled her onward.

Jonas patted her shoulder. "Pondering helps to keep this darkness in proper perspective. Have you heard of my namesake Jonas, or Jonah, as he was more often called?"

"Was he not the prophet who was swallowed by a large fish?"

"Yes, that was his punishment for not heeding the call from the Lord to preach repentance in Nineveh. Jonah tried to avoid it by boarding a ship to another city."

"It is swampy here," Mathoni said suddenly. "There must be a break in the stream. It may be slippery. Jael, you had better let go of my cloak and hold onto Jonas with both hands."

Jael clasped her arms around Jonas' waist. With each step, her feet sank deeper into the mud until it oozed past her ankles. The smell of rotting logs and mildew merged with the dense vapors in her nose. As she lifted her dress to keep it clean, she noticed the brush of filmy ferns against her legs. Then Mathoni begin to chuckle.

"What have you found to laugh at now?" Jonas asked.

"Listen. The three of us sound as if we are an enormous creature stalking its prey in the swamp."

As their feet sucked and sloshed through the mud, Jael grinned. Were she not so tired, she may have laughed out loud. It was good of Mathoni to point out the humor. She wondered why it had taken so long for her to appreciate that about him.

Soon the ground became solid again. Jael lowered her skirt and said, "I remember now about Jonah: A tempest arose on the sea, and he admitted to the other seamen that he had failed to heed the call from God."

"He told them to throw him into the sea," added her cousin. "But the Lord had prepared a great fish to swallow Jonah, and for three days he stayed in the belly of that fish. His experience parallels our three days in the darkness."

"I am not certain darkness was Jonah's chief concern in the belly of that fish," mused Mathoni. "The smell being only one of them!"

"Not something that would stimulate an appetite," agreed Jonas.

"Speaking of smell, we have reached another fence. I hope we shall not find more dead cattle."

Jael sniffed the air. No smell of death. Just the oppressive, bitter vapor. After hearing Mathoni's cloak swish over, she found a good handhold and scaled the weathered timbers. Then once again she caught hold of his cloak.

Jonas' arm found her shoulder. "During the time Jonah spent in the belly of the fish, he had time to ponder and learn, just as we are supposed to during these three days of darkness."

"Forgive me for stopping you again," Mathoni broke in, "but there is a fallen tree, and I am not certain whether to go around it or over it." He moved away momentarily, then returned and said, "There is a place to our right where the branches are bare enough that we can climb over the trunk." Mathoni took Jael's hand and led her carefully between branches and limbs lying on the ground. "This tree is larger than the last one you climbed over, so try to be a little less independent, all right?"

"All right." Jael smiled as Mathoni heaved himself over.

"Now, Jonas, give her a little boost to get her started, and I shall take it from there."

Jael clutched a limb and pulled herself upward while Jonas kept a steady hand on her back. Mathoni found her shoulders, then slid his hands down her sides to grip her waist and lift her down. "Thank you," she said as her sandals touched the ground.

Mathoni took in a breath as if he might speak. Yet he remained silent and merely ran his hands up and down her back. Her shawl slipped off one shoulder, but she did not attempt to fix it. When Jonas landed beside them, Mathoni quickly released his hold. Jael sighed, adjusted her shawl, and wondered what Mathoni had been thinking. Then she once again snatched hold of his cloak and let him lead her forward with Jonas at her side.

The soil became rocky, wrenching her knees and jabbing at her feet. Ignoring the pain, she faithfully followed the thud of Mathoni's stick and footsteps. She trusted him now. And that brought a peaceful lift to her heart.

A thorn scratched the hand she held the bedroll with. She pulled it closer to her side. "Jonas, a while ago you said we are supposed to learn something, as Jonah did, during the darkness."

"All of God's dealings with His children are to prepare them to be in His presence." Jonas sounded like his father at the pulpit in the synagogue. "Darkness is a symbol of separation from God and a lack of righteous living. In vapors such as we are in, people begin to repent and hunger for light, which is symbolic of truth, knowledge, and righteousness. When the darkness in this land comes to an end, the Lord Jesus Christ, the Light of the World, will appear. During these three days of darkness we must prepare to be in His presence."

Jael stared into the endless vapor. "How can preparations be made in this darkness?"

"It is not a temporal preparation, but a preparation of the heart, mind, and spirit. When Christ appears, we must be ready to humbly receive Him into our lives."

NINE

As Jael walked onward, her foot brushed a tuft of grass. She thought about the simple struggle the grass had, toiling to grow despite the tempest that had ravaged the land—so much like her own faith, straining against the dark fears in her mind. She longed to be as firmly rooted in spiritual matters as Jonas. "How shall we recognize Jesus when He appears?"

"Not with your eyes, but with your whole soul," said Jonas.

"And through the whisperings of the Spirit," added Mathoni.

Jael raised her eyes toward his voice. "Last night you said you knew nothing of the whisperings of the Spirit."

"I say many things I do not mean."

"Such as when you tease me?"

"Yes."

Jael wanted to catch up and link her arm through his. "Why did you become such a tease?"

"Perhaps as a protection against a heart that aches each time I confront pain and suffering." Mathoni was silent for a moment, then added, "Laughter is often better medicine than any salves or herbs I could use in restoring people's health."

Jael nodded in silent agreement and decided she could use more laughter in her life. Perhaps that would even help to cure Mother. Dear, frail Mother. Jael's fingers grasped Mathoni's cloak more firmly as she blindly followed him. After a while, she felt a change beneath her feet: the grass, which had been sporadic and clumped, now seemed to be laid out in a smooth field. She also noticed a faint fragrance of springtime here, despite the black vapors.

Mathoni abruptly stopped walking and Jael bumped into him. "Hah! That was fun."

"What?" asked Jonas.

"Nothing. Mathoni is teasing me again."

"That is not why I stopped. And, forgive me. I do not mean to laugh at your expense." Mathoni thumped his stick against the ground. "I stopped because, from here, I believe the stream goes through a series of grainfields like this one we are crossing. Walking through the seedlings is easier than much of the ground we have covered. If we abide here a while, long enough to partake of something to eat, perhaps we shall not have to stop until we feel the need to sleep again."

"Sleep again?" asked Jael. "Shall we not reach my house today?"

"How far do you think we have come?"

She stared into the darkness. "Would that I knew. Jonas, what do you think?"

"Less than halfway to the river."

Mathoni gently took Jael by one elbow. "There are some boulders here beside the stream. Sit down, and I shall find something in my satchel for us to eat."

"Thank you." Jael let him ease her down on a boulder. The rock was cold, contrasting with Mathoni's warm hand on her arm. Yet his hand did not remain there long. He set his satchel beside her and rustled through it. Jonas sat a few feet away and began gnawing on something.

"Here, see how you like this." Mathoni handed Jael something sticky.

"What is it?" She put a small piece in her mouth.

"My own creation. I call it scary berries. It is made from elderberries and blackberries, cooked together and mixed with honey, then dried in the sun. I gather the berries in the hills each autumn. It has become a favorite of wounded soldiers on the battlefield. Would you like to try some, Jonas?"

"I have tried it. Far too scary for my taste."

"What do you think, Jael?"

"With honey, I thought it would be sweet. Yet it makes my mouth pucker." She tried another piece. "But I like it."

"You must be very hungry," said Jonas. "I would not eat that unless it was my only hope of surviving on the battlefield."

"Hah! Now I know why it has become a favorite of wounded soldiers!" Mathoni ripped a loaf and gave some bread to Jael. "Let me know if you need some wine to wash it all down."

"That is one blessing of this darkness," said Jonas. "If we were walking in the sunshine, we would have to carry much more to drink."

"I would still rather walk in the light," said Jael.

"That is because you are not the one carrying the supplies." Mathoni took a swig from the flask.

"Forgive me. I do not mean to be a burden. But remember, it was not my idea for you to accompany me home."

Mathoni laid a hand on her shoulder. "It was my idea. And I have not regretted it." He gently massaged her shoulder.

Jael relaxed under his potent, yet tender, touch. "Are you still concerned that your sister needs your medical skills?"

His hand tensed, but he remained silent.

Jonas asked, "What are the two of you talking about?"

Jael let Mathoni provide the answer. "This darkness seems to have a strange effect on me. Just yesterday I said I had not learned to rely on the workings of the Spirit. Perhaps that is no longer true." He paused to take another drink from the flask.

"Go on," urged Jonas.

"I have this feeling, this prompting, that my medical skills are greatly needed, and I fear it involves my sister's family."

"Have you prayed about it?" Jonas persisted.

"You are the prayerful one here."

Jonas did not respond. Jael heard Mathoni chewing, then he swallowed but spoke no further. She finished the bread and berries then folded her anxious hands in her lap. The silence thickened. She stood. "If you two will excuse me."

"Take my stick with you for company," Mathoni said.

Jael paused before answering. It was hard to tell, without seeing his mischievous green eyes, if he was teasing or not. She finally decided he was not. "Thank you. Though I shall not be nearly as proficient with it as you." She rapped the stick along the ground and walked back along their trampled path through the six-inch high grain.

"It is not necessary to go far," Mathoni called. "We can see nothing in this darkness."

Jael winced at his comment but continued until sure she was a comfortable distance away. Then she moved a few steps off the trail, took care of her needs, and stood up. But she arose too quickly. Her head swam. She clutched the stick with both hands. She leaned her forehead against it and tried to breathe deeply and evenly. The dizziness finally subsided. Yet now she was no longer sure which direction to go to return to the others. She squinted into the syrupy vapor. Her fingernails dug into the stick. She listened, hoping to hear the splash of water in the stream or Jonas' and Mathoni's voices. Yet all she heard was the increasing drum of her heart.

Then something else came to her ears. Not voices, nor the sound of water; not even the rumble of an earthquake. It was the snorting and sniffing of an animal on the prowl. Jael froze. She heard the pawing of footprints, drawing closer by the second. Though veiled to her view, she knew the animal could smell her. She quickly conjured the vision of a puma—a hungry one, at that—with its teeth bared, ready to pounce.

A shriek erupted from her throat like a blare of trumpets, calling warriors to battle. And that was what ensued. Jonas and Mathoni raced forward to confront whatever danger had jeopardized her safety.

"Jael?" Jonas called. "What is it? What is the matter?"

"Jael!" boomed Mathoni's voice, getting nearer. "Calm down. Stop screaming, for mercy's sake!"

But rather than calming, Jael began to wield the stick, slashing it insanely in every direction. It whacked against something solid, jarring her senses. Then it was roughly jerked from her hands.

"Ow!" she cried, wincing at the pain.

"'Ow!' is right!" Mathoni bellowed, then he caught her in a tight grasp. "What are you trying to do? Calm down, will you?"

Jael continued to fight, straining against his muscled arms and beating her fists upon his chest.

"Calm down. I am not going to hurt you. Everything is all right." Mathoni held her flailing body until all the fight was gone.

Jael slumped against him while shudders of fear twinged through her. The warmth of his cloak covered her shoulders.

"Jonas, she has lost her shawl somewhere. Will you try to find it?" Vaguely, she heard her cousin drop to the ground and search for the lost shawl.

"Are you strong enough to walk?" Mathoni asked in a kind tone. "Just a little ways, back to sit on the boulder."

"Not yet," her voice rasped.

"I found the shawl!" Jonas exclaimed. "Do you want it?"

"In a moment," said Mathoni.

Closing her eyes, she rested her head against his deerskin vest and tried to draw strength from the steady pulsing of his heart. His fingers stroked her long hair. Then he leaned his cheek against the top of her head. A delicate warmth spread from there downward until it reached her feet.

"Nice," said his hushed voice in her ear.

"Is there something I can do?" Jonas said, interrupting their caress.

"Not a thing," said Mathoni as he gently rubbed her back.

"I am all right now," Jael said, wishing she could stay there forever drawing solace from his embrace.

"We shall go back to the boulder." Mathoni secured one arm around her waist, then his stick began to tap. Jael held onto the edge of his vest and moved slowly forward.

Jonas came up behind them. "What happened, Jael? What frightened you so?"

Jael shuddered once more. The animal was still concealed in the black vapors.

Mathoni pulled her closer to his side. "You are trembling. Please tell us why you are so afraid."

She gripped his vest more securely. What she wanted was to forget about it; or better yet, hope it was only her imagination. Mathoni seated her on the boulder and took his cloak while Jonas laid the shawl upon on her shoulders. Then she drew in a quivering breath and prepared to speak.

But Jonas beat her to it. "Shoo!" he shouted, whipping his cloak through the murky air. "Get away, whatever you are!"

"What is it?" asked Mathoni.

"A dog, I think. It has been eating my dried venison."

"Smart dog," said Mathoni. "I am glad I left our meat tied up in my satchel."

"The poor animal is so hungry it will not leave, no matter how hard I hit it with my cloak. Perhaps, Mathoni, you should offer it some of your scary berries to scare it away."

"Hah!" laughed Mathoni.

The tension in Jael evaporated as humor took over. She began to giggle, not merely at her companions' words, but also at her own misdirected fears.

"Jael?" Mathoni laid his hands on her shoulders. "Are you crying?"

"No, I am laughing." She allowed her shoulders to shake freely with mirth.

"That is a first," said Mathoni. "What brought this on?"

"My own foolishness." She placed a hand on top of his.

"That dog . . . that is what all my screaming was about. I thought it was a wild animal ready to attack me."

"Come here, fellow," Jonas said. "You may as well finish off the venison. I cannot eat it now that you have mangled it." The dog whimpered and came closer. "There you go. Eat hearty."

The dog chewed hungrily at his feast. Jael smiled. "You are right, Mathoni. Laughter is beneficial in certain situations."

He knelt behind her, wrapped his arms around her shoulders, and leaned his cheek against her ear. "Darkness is also beneficial in certain situations."

Jael tipped back her head, resting it on his shoulder. No longer would she wonder how Mathoni felt about her. It was clear that he meant to be a shield and comfort to her. Just to hear his quiet breathing near her ear soothed away all her fears. Never before had she felt so secure, so protected—even from the bitter black mist that had weighed upon her for hours.

Jonas' voice rose through the darkness. "This dog is still a puppy—a rather large puppy, but he seems quite harmless. And I fear he expects me to continue feeding him."

Mathoni lifted his head. "Perhaps you could send him to find that herd of dead cattle. Plenty of fresh meat there!"

His words quickly dissolved the tender caress. "Oh, please, Mathoni!" Jael groaned. "That is an awful thought."

"And I believe even the dumbest animal would be repelled by the odor there," said Jonas.

Mathoni's hand brushed Jael's arm as he picked up his satchel. "We should be moving on."

"I suppose I have just acquired a new pet. Perhaps he will prove useful on our journey." Jonas came toward Jael as he spoke. The dog also neared, sniffed at her, and licked her hand. She patted his head then reached for her bedroll and stood up.

Mathoni pulled her to his side. "Here, Jonas, take my stick and lead. I shall keep Jael beside me to give you a rest."

"I have no need of a rest. Jael is my cousin. I feel

responsible for her."

"As do I. Your father commanded me to get her safely home."

He anchored his arm around her waist. "With the Spirit to guide you, Jonas, and that dog at your side, you shall be a much better leader than I in this darkness."

"Not if this dog is like the one your brother used to have. He was afraid of everything."

"Hah! Not afraid of everything. Just of cows." Mathoni pulled Jael's arm securely behind his waist. "If you hang onto me, you shall be less likely to stumble."

She began to walk at his side through the grainfield. "Why would a dog be afraid of cows?"

"When he was but a puppy, he was kicked by a cow while Mathonihah was milking." Mathoni chuckled. "Not only did it make him afraid of cows, but he would never come near a pot of milk. If my mother wanted to keep him out of the house, she merely placed a pot or bowl of milk at the door."

"I find that hard to believe."

"No, it is true," confirmed Jonas. "I have never known such a fearful creature in my life."

Jael smiled and recalled her own fear of the unknown animal. She touched the sheathed sword, tied to the sash at Mathoni's waist. "I am glad you did not have to use this back there."

"To wield away the ferocious animal that came after you? Hah! You did a fine job of fending for yourself. You are quite a threat with a stick in your hands. You whacked me a good one across the thighs. I shall be bruised for weeks!"

"Oh, Mathoni, forgive me!" Jael briefly leaned her cheek against his muscled arm.

"I am not letting you out of my sight again."

It was Jael's turn to laugh. "When have I been in your sight in this darkness?"

"Hah! Now who is becoming the tease?"

"Just giving you a taste of your own medicine."

"I am the physician. Let me handle the medicine." Mathoni tightened his hold around her waist, then he became silent, and Jael wondered where his thoughts were taking him. Up ahead, she heard the steady panting of the dog and the rapping of the stick Jonas carried. Though her feet were constantly in motion, she knew they were making little progress.

After a while, Jonas halted to warn them of obstacles in the way. "I am not sure what we have come upon. Perhaps rubble from a fallen house or some other structure. There are timbers and beams lying every which way on the ground."

Mathoni's body stiffened beside Jael. "Shall we try to go through it or around it?" Suddenly the dog began to whine and trot in a circle around them. "What is wrong with him?"

"Perhaps it is better not to know," said Jael.

TEN

"Jael, stay here with Jonas," Mathoni said firmly.

She heard him scramble through the clutter. The whimpering dog followed. A strange odor in the thick air reminded her of the night her father died. She pushed the sad thoughts aside and listened to Mathoni's clattering and crunching in the darkness.

"It is a house," he said after a moment. "From the way the dog is behaving, I assume it is where he lived."

"Do you need my help?" Jonas asked.

"No." Mathoni's voice was further away.

When Jael heard nothing more for several minutes she called out, "Mathoni? Are you all right?"

"Yes!" His voice was stiff. "Would that I could say the same for the people who owned the dog."

"Is there anything we can do?" Jonas asked.

"Nothing." Mathoni's voice came closer. "It is just so senseless, all this death and destruction. I found five people, one of them a small child, lying beside the doorway, as if they were about to flee outside. But the house collapsed and killed them all before they had a chance."

"They had a chance," Jonas said in a somber voice. "A chance to repent. The Lord has promised to spare the righteous."

"But a child!" Mathoni's voice echoed through the brutal blackness. "How could God kill an innocent child?"

Jael's hand crushed the bedroll. What a sad ending to this family! She longed to reach out to console Mathoni. Yet he never came near enough, and she did not trust herself to move through the debris toward him. She breathed a long sigh.

Jonas picked up her hand. "The child is only dead to the things of this world. Every innocent child will be saved in the kingdom of heaven."

"That sounds perfect in theory," murmured Mathoni, "but it does not make this situation any easier to accept." He came to Jael's side and found Jonas there. "Where is my stick? I shall again take the lead while the two of you walk together."

Jael's heart wanted to object, but her head said Mathoni needed to be alone. "Where is the dog?" she asked. "We cannot leave him here."

"No. There is nothing for him here," said Mathoni. "He will follow us when we leave."

"Which way do you intend to go?" Jonas took Jael more firmly by the hand.

"The stream is only a short distance to our left, so we shall have to skirt around the house to our right. There may be sheds or storehouses nearby, which will make our passing more perilous. And surely, we will come across other houses."

"Let us pray we will find better circumstances," said Jonas.

"You pray while I lead." Mathoni's stick thudded heavily as he moved onward.

The dog came panting up behind Jael and Jonas. He seemed content enough to follow them and leave the deceased family behind. Jael tried to imagine the color of his fur. "I wonder if he has a name."

"He is young enough that he could learn to answer to a new name," said Jonas. "Do you have one in mind?"

"Orphan," Mathoni said bluntly.

"Oh, Mathoni!" Jael moaned. "Surely we can come up with a more pleasant name." The dog barked, as if agreeing with her. "Give me a while and I shall think of one." The dog's barking intensified. Then he ran off through the darkness.

"What is he doing?" asked Jonas.

"Rounding up sheep," said Mathoni. "Listen and you shall hear them. I can also smell them. That dog was trained to work with sheep, and he is merely rounding up his herd."

"I hope he does not expect me to feed them," mused Jonas.

Jael heard their bleating in the distance. "At least they are not dead, like the cattle."

"No," said her cousin. "They seemed to have lived through the tempest and earthquakes."

"Better than their keepers did," said Mathoni gruffly.

Jael groped her way onward behind him. Dozens of times each year she had made this trek to and from Uncle Nephi's. But never in her life had she fought against such endless darkness. It weighed on her like massive chains. Was this comparable to the chains of hell, she wondered, which Uncle Nephi had warned the people of in his preachings?

"There are piles of mud bricks and other debris scattered here," Mathoni said. "Move to your right."

Jael stubbed her toe and whimpered. When Jonas slipped an arm around her waist to help her along, she wished it was Mathoni's arm. Yet he remained in his own thoughts, perhaps still pondering the demise of the dog's owners. Jael could understand his intense desire to ease people's pain and suffering. Mother was that way, foregoing her own needs to stay at a woman's beside, sometimes for several days. Perhaps that was why Mother had grown so frail in recent years. Mother! Fear pricked Jael's heart. Would that she could be home this instant!

The dog came barking towards them. Jael bent down and ran her hands through his fur, thick and wavy, but still of an unknown color. "Did you give up trying to herd your sheep?"

"He seemed to easily find his way back to us in the darkness," said Jonas. "Perhaps we should name him Liahona. He may help us find our way, as the Liahona helped to guide our forefathers through the wilderness."

"Liahona," mused Jael. "That is the name of the strange ball

Uncle Nephi keeps in the box with the brass plates."

"When did you see the Liahona?"

"Samuel showed me once. But he was too young to tell me of its purpose."

"The Liahona is something like a compass, with two spindles which point the direction of travel. It was prepared by the Lord to guide Lehi and his family to the Promised Land after they left Jerusalem. But they soon discovered it only worked when they were righteous and exercised faith in the Lord."

"Next you shall tell us that the dog was prepared by the Lord to guide us," said Mathoni.

"Whether we realize it or not, the Lord has a hand in much of the good that occurs in our lives," said Jonas. "Perhaps this dog will turn out to be a bless . . ." He stopped as the dog began to yowl. "Is something amiss, Liahona? Or do you not like us talking about you?" The yowl turned into a whine. Then the dog tried to squeeze between Jael and Jonas.

"Is he warning us about s—" The earth began to groan and sway. Jael clutched her cousin. The dog huddled closely beside their legs. The tremor made Jael's stomach tighten, and she was glad when it ended quickly.

Jonas once again took her hand and they slowly followed Mathoni through the mists of darkness. After a time they discovered a short stone wall. On the other side was a recently-plowed field, and the upturned earth made walking difficult. Each step wrenched Jael's knees and ankles, and she wondered how long she would have to endure the rugged ground.

"It is time to leave the stream," Mathoni said, as if in answer to her unspoken thought. "I believe there is a road nearby which parallels the stream and leads to the river."

"The same inspiration also came to me," said Jonas.

"I'm not claiming it's inspiration," Mathoni declared.

Jael reached out to touch his arm. He jerked away and trudged to their right through the plowed field. Jael hugged the bedroll against her chest. The feelings they had shared earlier seemed now as erratic as the ground beneath her feet.

For a long while they traveled in silence, with only an occasional bark from Liahona. At Mathoni's direction, Jonas steered Jael around fallen structures along the way. And finally, Mathoni announced that they had reached the highway.

"I hope it is not like the highway in town," said Jael, "with a crevice down the middle."

"Here the highway is not stone slabs, but merely dirt," replied Mathoni. "We should make better progress now."

"Anything is better than that plowed field," said Jonas.

They had not gone more than a hundred steps before the earth began to quake again. Though only a slight tremor, it caused Jael to ask, "Why are the earthquakes returning?"

"I have asked myself the same question. The only answer I have is that there may be more wickedness here. I believe we are near the village where Father, Uncle Timothy, and others of us tried in vain to call the people to repentance."

Jonas helped Jael over some fallen timbers. "I shall never forget that experience. I was sixteen. Father had recently ordained me to preach the gospel. And here, the people were quite hostile—angry enough that they began throwing stones to chase us away."

"Was that when Uncle Timothy was stoned to death?"

"Yes. It was a blessing that others were not also killed."

"Stop! Go back!" Mathoni suddenly bellowed. "It is not safe here. There is a deep crevice in the earth, and the edges of it are unstable."

"What shall we do?" Jael asked.

"I am not certain. We cannot leap over this one." Mathoni stepped back beside Jonas. "And you claimed your dog would help us find our way."

"It is not as though he could smell a hole in the ground."

"Or that the Spirit could warn you?" Mathoni muttered.

"If you had been leading with the Spirit, perhaps we would have avoided this place entirely," Jonas hastily said.

"So now you are calling me to repentance?" shouted Mathoni.

"And you are going to stone me?" Jonas shouted back.

Jael dug her fingernails into the bedroll. She had grown used to Mathoni's abrasiveness. But it was rare for Jonas to say anything harsh. She tried to think of soothing words to pacify her companions. Yet her weary mind would not allow it. The silence strained through her like gauzy cobwebs. She felt Jonas' palm perspiring against hers and heard Mathoni pounding his stick against the dirt.

Finally, she pried her mouth open. "Would you like me to help you look for stones, Mathoni? They may be hard to find in this darkness." She forced herself to giggle, and soon both Jonas and Mathoni began to laugh with her.

"Forgive me," said Jonas as he patted Mathoni on the back. "I have let my pride come between us. I should never have said what I did about your leading without the Spirit—as if I were the only one entitled to inspiration."

"I may be rather a new believer in the workings of the Spirit, but you should give me some credit for not leading you headlong into the crevice."

"Yes, I should."

"Thank you, Jael," said Mathoni, "for helping us laugh at the situation. That is usually my role. I guess I temporarily lost my sense of humor."

"That happened yesterday when you were tired," she said.

"Oh?" Mathoni laid a solid hand on her shoulder. "So you think it is time we found shelter where we might sleep?"

Jael felt a warm glow inside. "It is up to you."

"I would prefer to cross through this particular area before we stop," said Jonas.

"Then we must first get around or across this crevice."

Mathoni released his grasp on Jael's shoulder.

"We should simply span the chasm with some timbers, or perhaps a door," said Jonas.

"I am not sure it would be that simple. You have not probed the depth of the chasm with the stick nor stood on its precarious edges as I have."

"No, but I am about to," said Jonas. "Let me use the stick, Mathoni."

"Be careful," Jael said as her cousin moved away.

"No need to worry. He is in tune with the Spirit." Mathoni came to her side. "And to think I was about to stone him."

"Not so!"

"Hah!" He slipped his arms around her waist. "I believe you were right in observing that the worst in me comes out when I am tired."

"You must be tired often," she said in jest.

"Hah! You are becoming quite a tease! And I like it." Mathoni hugged her against his broad chest. "There are many things I am learning to like about you."

Their embrace was brief. Jonas soon returned, and together they spanned the crevice with timbers from a fallen building. Mathoni took his stick and went ahead to test the strength of their bridge, then called for them to come across. Jael put one foot on a narrow timber and the next foot on the adjacent timber. Jonas steadied her with a hand on her back. Sliding her feet slowly forward, she wondered if it was a blessing or curse to not see the depth of the crevice beneath her. The bedroll pulled awkwardly on her shoulder as she teetered her way across. She started when Mathoni grabbed her arm.

"There you go," he said, pulling her to his side. He then handed the stick to Jonas. "You may lead again, my friend."

Jael smiled and laid her cheek against Mathoni's arm.

"Are you weary?" he asked.

"Yes. Shall we search for a shelter to sleep in?"

"I feel uneasy about staying in this part of the land."

"Because of what Jonas said?"

"The last thing I would want is for someone to come along and stone you."

"Is there more to it than that?"

"Do you realize that we have been traveling near a village for some time, and we have heard no voices but our own?"

ELEVEN

Jael tucked her thumb around the sash at Mathoni's waist and tried to keep pace with his lengthy stride. "Yesterday you were concerned about hearing too many voices, and today you are worried about hearing none?"

Mathoni did not answer. He briefly let go of her and readjusted the satchel on his opposite shoulder. Then he pulled her so close that their thighs brushed while walking.

Jael took in the scent of his deerskin vest. And she listened to the flutter of his cloak behind him as he moved. "Are you still concerned about your sister?"

"The closer we get to the river, the more anxious I become, which is why this silence disturbs me. I would rather know that people are alive and wounded and perhaps curable than to know they have died with no hope of restoration."

"There is always hope," Jonas said from up ahead.

"Through performing a miracle," said Jael, "such as when Uncle Timothy was raised from the dead?"

"There is always hope, whether in this life or the next."

"But Jonas, sometimes hope is not enough. Since the turmoil began I have prayed that Mother is all right. But until I see her and know for certain, I cannot be at peace." Jael felt Mathoni's arm grip her waist more firmly. How she valued the strength he offered to help her carry on!

"There are an increasing number of small crevices here," Jonas announced. "We shall have to go even slower for a while."

Jael began to tentatively slide her feet. The process became tedious, tiring, and she longed for a diversion. "Jonas, would you tell me of the day Uncle Timothy was stoned to death?"

"Certainly." Jonas thudded the stick as he slowly moved forward. "While I was with Father, Uncle Timothy, and a few other brethren, the people reviled against our teachings. They demanded that we leave their synagogue and threatened our lives. We found refuge with my mother's sister, Ruth, and her husband Shemnon. Then at sunset, Father decided we must try again to convince the people of the error in their ways."

"If the people were wicked enough to force you from their synagogue," interrupted Mathoni, "why did you not simply leave and go elsewhere to preach?"

"Would that the choice had been mine," Jonas said soberly. "I have learned from Father that it is not our own will, but the Lord's will, which must be heeded. That day, I watched Father and Uncle Timothy go forth preaching with power and performing many miracles. They cast out devils and healed many people of infirmities. And though everyone witnessed God's almighty power, Satan maintained his hold upon their hearts, and they began throwing stones to drive us away. Uncle Timothy was hit in the head, and he fell dead at my feet."

"Are you certain he was dead?" asked Mathoni.

"That sounds like a question my doubtful friend would ask."

"I am a physician. I deal with life and death constantly."

"So do prophets of God. Yet their concern is not with temporal, but spiritual life and death."

"You failed to answer my question."

"Timothy was dead."

"How do you know? Were you not fleeing for your own life?"

"Yes. But I stopped when Uncle Timothy fell, though stones continued to fly around us." Jonas let Jael and Mathoni come up beside him. "Never have I seen my father radiate so much power. His countenance became a brilliant white as he faced the angry mob. He commanded them in the name of Jesus Christ to cease their stoning. He testified that he had been called of God to preach repentance and remission of sins that they might desire to be baptized. Some heckled him and said that Father was not the chief judge and had no jurisdiction over them. Yet he continued to stand forth and testify with power."

"Should we not keep walking?" asked Mathoni.

"Come, Liahona, let us move on."

Jael again began to slide her feet along the unpredictable terrain. "Please, Jonas, finish what you were saying."

"All the while Father faced the mob, I held Uncle Timothy. Blood poured from a large wound on his head. Soon he went completely limp in my arms. By the time the mob dispersed and Father came to join us, Uncle Timothy had quit breathing. I laid him on the ground and put my head against his chest. There was no heartbeat. I remember feeling that my own heart might also stop. Only recently had I been ordained to the ministry. I failed to understand why the Lord would not protect us while doing His work. And I could not believe that people could be so cruel to one another."

Mathoni took in a deep breath. "You had a glimpse of what I face constantly on the battlefield."

"Yes, I did. Then I had a glimpse of what the power of the Lord can do. My father laid his hands on Uncle Timothy's head, and, in the name of the Lord, commanded his spirit to return to his body. Immediately his heartbeat was restored and he began to breathe. We did what we could to bind his bleeding wound, then the two of us carried him back to the house of Shemnon and Ruth, who cared for him until he was strong enough to travel home."

"And you believe it was the power of the Lord that restored Timothy's life?" asked Mathoni.

"My father is not a physician—not skilled in the use of medicine and herbs, as your father is. But he does know how to use the gifts of the Spirit."

Mathoni took in a long, deep breath. "Would that I could use such gifts in my life."

"You only think it would make you a better physician if you could cure people miraculously," said Jonas.

"It would make me a better man," Mathoni said firmly.

Jael remained silent, but her footsteps were lighter as she pondered how Mathoni's doubtful heart was stretching heavenward. She also sensed her own heart enlarging within her breast.

"A great sign!" Jonas exclaimed. "The road has turned from dirt to stones, which means we have come to the center of the village. If we continue from here, in a few minutes we should find the synagogue, which will be an ideal shelter to rest in."

"Is this not the synagogue you were thrown out of?"

"The synagogue was once dedicated as a house of God. Though perhaps for a time the people defiled it, I am sure the recent storms have cleansed and purified it once more."

"I am in agreement that we should rest," said Mathoni. "My arm has grown tired of holding this cousin of yours on her feet."

"I thought I was holding you up," she said.

"Hah!"

Jael followed Jonas' tapping along the pavement with Liahona panting nearby. The air seemed heavier with more smoky and rancid smells. It took a great deal of concentration to not twist her ankles on the stones left askew by the earthquakes. Growing increasingly weary, she slumped against Mathoni.

Liahona began to whine and Jonas tried to quiet him.

A high-pitched screech stunned Jael's ears, then another and another. Something whirred near her head. Mathoni jerked and ducked. "What is it?" she asked, nestling closer to his side.

"Bats." He raised a hand to shield Jael's forehead.

"There must be hundreds," said Jonas. "They are driving Liahona mad."

"They are driving me mad," said Mathoni.

"But how can they fly in this darkness?" Jael asked.

"Bats do not have to see to navigate," answered Jonas. "They use screeching and their ears to guide them."

Mathoni ducked again. "Perhaps we could learn something from their technique." Suddenly he let out a gravelly shriek. Jael started. "Forgive me," he said. "I did not mean to frighten you."

Liahona began a lengthy wail. "Now see what you started, Mathoni," complained Jonas. "Stop it, Liahona. You will wake the dead with your howling."

"Hah!" laughed Mathoni. "From the smell here, I would say there are plenty of dead to be awakened."

"Oh please, Mathoni!" Jael moaned, shaking her head.

"You and Liahona seem to have scared the bats away," said Jonas, rapping his stick along the stone pavement.

Mathoni tightened his grasp at Jael's waist and urged her slowly onward. Drained, emotionally and physically, Jael was ready to rest in whatever shelter they might find.

"We should be nearing the synagogue by now," Jonas said. "If I could just find the courtyard wall."

"You have both amazed me," Jael said softly, "in finding your way through this darkness. I would be lost without you."

Tipping his head against hers, Mathoni whispered, "And I would be lonesome without you."

Jonas' tapping stopped. "Here we are." An iron gate creaked open, and Mathoni led Jael through it. She leaned heavily against him as they crossed the courtyard.

"I found the door," said Jonas, as Liahona began a furious bark. "Hush, you noisy pup!" he commanded, but Liahona continued to bark. Then, from within the synagogue came the vicious growl of another dog. "It sounds as though you have met your match, Liahona." Jonas spoke from near the ground as if he had knelt beside the dog.

"What is a dog doing inside the synagogue?" asked

Mathoni. "You said the storms and earthquakes would have purified it."

"Perhaps its owners have taken shelter inside," said Jonas.

Mathoni pulled away from Jael. "Jonas, give me back the stick and remain here to hold Liahona, while I go inside and see what I can find."

Jael longed to stay at his side. "And what of me?"

"I would prefer you abide here with Jonas."

"I would prefer to go inside with you."

"Are you certain?"

"What is so fearful about a dog?" she asked.

"The dog is what we know of. What is fearful are the things we are uncertain of."

"With the proper amount of faith, there is never a need to fear," advised Jonas.

"Yes, I am sure that is true." Mathoni leaned forward and gave the door a gentle shove. The growling on the other side magnified. "Hold onto my cloak, Jael, while I nudge the dog with the stick."

Her nervous hands clutched his cloak. She heard the door swing open, then the cloak tugged her forward into the dank-smelling synagogue. The dog's growls turned to whimpers, and it quickly retreated to a distant corner. Jael heard voices from the same direction.

"Hello? Is someone there?" Mathoni called through the dark vapor. Then he brought Jael to his side.

"Yes," answered a man's voice. "A score of us have taken shelter here. Our homes were destroyed in the earthquakes."

"I am Mathoni, son of Zedekiah the physician."

"Mathoni?" asked a woman. "Are you not a friend to my sister's son Jonas?"

"Yes, Jonas is my friend."

"Do you have word of Rachel and her husband Nephi?"

"I have better than words. I have brought Jonas with me. He

is outside. He can tell you of his family." Mathoni called over his shoulder, "Jonas, come inside. But tie your sash around Liahona's neck to restrain him." The door creaked, and Mathoni turned to speak with Jonas as he stepped inside. "Your mother's sister is here."

"Aunt Ruth? Aunt Ruth!" Jonas shouted. "Is Uncle Shemnon with you?"

"Yes, as are our children and a few neighbors."

Jonas rushed forth in the direction of his aunt's voice. Jael heard the clicking of Liahona's feet against the mosaic floor. Mathoni tapped with his stick and urged Jael between the benches toward the front of the synagogue.

"Uncle Shemnon!" exclaimed Jonas. "Aunt Ruth! I am pleased you are alive and well."

Jael sensed the fervor in Jonas' embracing of his aunt and uncle. A hunger to clasp her mother roamed through her like a slow-acting poison, weakening her travel-weary body. She drooped against Mathoni's strong arm.

"Why are the two of you traveling in this darkness?" asked Shemnon.

"There are three of us," answered Jonas. "We are taking my cousin Jael home to be with her mother. Also we must see about other relatives in this part of the land. Father has asked me to tell everyone to assemble at the temple after the light returns to make an accounting of those who remain alive."

"Why at the temple?" asked Ruth.

"It is prophesied that sometime after the darkness fades Jesus Christ will appear to the righteous people in this land. Father believes He will come to the temple."

"Yes, I recall the prophecies of the Lord's visit to this land," Shemnon said meekly.

"And what of your father and mother?" asked Ruth.

"They are well enough, though Father was slightly wounded by a rafter that fell. We were blessed to have Mathoni at our home to mend Father's shoulder."

"There are wounded among us," said Shemnon. "Perhaps Mathoni would share his skills here?"

"I shall do what I can to help," said Mathoni. "But first, I must secure a place for Jael to sleep."

A gentle wave of warmth washed through her. Mathoni truly was concerned for her welfare. And moreover, his attitude toward helping others had changed since their talk yesterday.

"Jonas," said Shemnon, "it was your father's brother who suggested we take refuge in the synagogue."

"Uncle Timothy?"

"Yes. Soon after the darkness overcame us, Timothy left his family and began to search out those who needed help." Shemnon cleared his throat. "Not many in this part of the land were spared from destruction. Just twenty of us, as far as we know."

Jael's voice quivered, "Did Uncle Timothy have word of my mother?"

"He gave us no word of your mother," answered Shemnon.

"May the good Lord grant that she is well," said Ruth.

Mathoni led Jael forward a few more steps. "Have you a place where Jael might lie down?"

"Yes." Ruth reached through the darkness for Jael, who let herself be pulled from Mathoni's grasp. Then Ruth led her toward a quiet spot in the synagogue. "You may sleep on my quilt."

"I have a bedroll." Jael held it forth for the woman to touch. "So I shall not be in your way when you need to rest."

"I have yet to do any resting. There is much to be done to feed and care for the wounded amongst my family and neighbors. With Mathoni here, perhaps I shall finally be able to rest."

"Mathoni has been well taught." Jael unrolled the quilted bedding. "But he has no medical supplies with him."

"I have roots and herbs for pain, but I am not skilled at

mending broken bones or closing deep wounds. We have a young father amongst us that I feared would die from his wounds. Now there is hope that he will live."

"Let us pray it will be so." Jael knelt upon the bedroll.

"Could I bring you something to eat or drink?"

"No, thank you. My only need now is to sleep." Jael stretched out on one side of the quilt and pulled the other side over her weary frame. "If you have food to spare, perhaps Mathoni and Jonas would like something to eat. We have been traveling for two days—at least, I think it has been two days."

"It is hard to know in this darkness." Ruth's footsteps slowly retreated. "Sleep well."

Jael drifted off quickly, but she was plagued with dreams that made her toss and turn. When Jonas and Mathoni came to roll out their bedding, one on each side of her, she slept more deeply, though the fearful dreams continued.

Hours later, she was awakened by a woman's screaming. Then she realized it was the cry of her own voice.

TWELVE

Mathoni and Jonas both seized Jael and tried to calm her, but she struggled against them—thinking they were part of her nightmare. "Mother!" she sobbed. "Mother, please do not die!"

"Jael, wake up!" Mathoni said in a hushed voice.

Tears streamed down her cheeks. Liahona, lying at her feet, began to bark.

"Quiet your dog, Jonas," demanded Mathoni. Jonas released his hold on Jael. Mathoni raised her off the bedroll and cradled her in his arms. "It was but a dream," he soothed.

"No," Jael wept. "Mother is dying. I must go to her."

Liahona sniffed at Jael then licked her hands covering her face. Something about the gentle lap of his tongue eased her fears. She pulled away from Mathoni and hugged her knees to her chest. "Forgive me. I did not mean to awaken you."

"Do you truly believe your mother is dying?" asked Jonas, lying down again. "Might it have been a vision, not a dream?"

Jael blotted her tears on the shawl. "I know nothing of visions."

Mathoni squeezed her shoulder, then his hand followed the curve of her arm until it rested on her hand. "I am prepared to travel on to the river, if that is what you wish to do."

Jonas moaned, "And I would prefer to sleep a while longer."

"Now you have become a murmurer," said Mathoni. "That is so unlike you, Jonas."

"Perhaps I have been with you too long."

"Please. I cannot bear to have you argue. This is my fault. Were it not for my need to get home, you could both be with your own families."

"That is not true." Mathoni stroked her hand. "Martha also lives on this side of the valley, and I have not slept well for thinking about her. I would soon like to continue our journey."

"All right," Jonas yawned, rising from his blanket. "Come, Liahona. Let us be on our way."

"Could I prepare you something to eat before you leave?" Ruth's voice came from a nearby corner.

"No, thank you, Aunt Ruth," answered Jonas. "We would not want to trouble you."

"Forgive us for disturbing your sleep," said Jael. "You have been kind to let us stay here with you."

"And you have been generous with your help. We shall pray for your safe journey," said Shemnon.

"And that your mother is well, Jael," added Ruth.

"Thank you." Jael crawled off her bedroll, smoothed it, and began to roll it up.

"I shall do that." Mathoni handed her a small loaf of bread. "You must eat this and some nuts and raisins, since you ate nothing before you went to sleep. It will give you strength for our journey."

"It is no wonder she had fearful dreams," said Jonas. "Sleeping with an empty stomach also does that to me."

"Perhaps I should try it," said Mathoni. "I might begin to have visions."

"Miracles happen," mused Jonas.

"Speaking of miracles," Mathoni began, "when you told us of the day Timothy was raised from the dead, you said your father's countenance shone. Is it possible that you inherited some of that radiance, so we might have light for our journey?"

"As I said, miracles happen. However, the gifts of the Spirit must be earned through righteous living."

"Give it a try," Mathoni said lightly. "It would be a blessing to actually see where we are going."

"The three days shall soon end," said Jonas.

"I wish we knew how soon," sighed Jael. She finished her meal and stood up. "Where is my bedroll?"

"I shall carry it today." Mathoni's arm anchored behind her waist. "Now that we have consumed most of our food, my satchel is near empty, and I have put your bedroll inside it." He led her across the synagogue with his stick rapping against the mosaic floor. Jonas and Liahona followed them out the door.

As Jael stepped through the courtyard, the horrid smell turned her stomach—much worse than the day before.

"The stench here is like a battlefield," said Mathoni. "I shall be glad to leave this village."

"If we go back to the highway, we should make good progress to Uncle Timothy's house," said Jonas. "Are you taking the lead, Mathoni? You are the one with the stick."

"You are the one with the dog," answered Mathoni. "And you know the way to Timothy's house better than I. So take my stick and keep Liahona at your side, while I keep Jael at mine."

"Perhaps some light is needed so I might keep my eye on the two of you?"

"Hah! Whatever for? I only want Jael at my side because she makes better conversation than your dog. Liahona merely whines and barks. But Jael is capable of weeping in sorrow, shouting in anger, and screaming in fear."

Jael bumped Mathoni with her hip, then wished she hadn't, because they both nearly fell on the fragmented pavement. It took longer than she expected to make their way back to the dirt highway. The entire journey had been like that. Her feet became more bruised, her legs constantly ached, and her lungs burned from inhaling the noxious vapors. She may never have left Uncle Nephi's if she had known how hard the trip would be.

"Stop! Stay where you are!" Jonas yelled, causing Liahona to bark. Mathoni jerked Jael to a halt. "Hush, Liahona!" demanded Jonas. "Your barking will not help in this situation."

Jael crumpled the bodice of her dress in her fist. Beneath the grasp came the profound thud of her heart. Vaguely, she heard Mathoni tell her to wait there while he went with Jonas to see what lay ahead. Liahona's barks turned into whines.

"Come here, Liahona," Jael called, eager for something to hold onto. "Come, Liahona." Bending low, she stepped forward, sweeping her hands through the darkness to find the dog. She touched fur, but not Liahona's. Her throat constricted. An eerie chill crept up her spine as she forced her hands to examine the animal lying on the roadway. Mane, ears, long forehead and snout. A horse—cold and dead. Jael's skin prickled. She stood and moved in the direction of Jonas' and Mathoni's voices.

"They might also be Lamanites," Jonas said.

"I still believe they are part of the Gadianton band of robbers," Mathoni replied.

Jael groped her way forward. "What have you found?"

"A small battalion of soldiers, with some horses as well as countless shields, spears, and other weapons." Mathoni reached for Jael's hand. "I believe the people and animals are all dead, though it is not because they were caught in buildings that collapsed or burned. They just died here on the open highway."

"But how?" she asked.

"Lightning, hailstones, or perhaps both," said Mathoni.

"God must work within the natural laws that govern the earth and heaven," said Jonas—his voice moving away.

"Feel this." Mathoni handed her a metal bar with something attached.

The object was heavier than she expected, and she nearly dropped it. "What is this? A shield?"

"Yes. Feel it and see if you can find anything unusual."

Jael ran a hand across the shield, which was longer than her forearm. The metal was rough and cratered, as if it had fended off hundreds of weapons. "It has many holes."

"Which perhaps is not so unusual after a lengthy battle.

Now feel this headplate." Mathoni took the shield and handed her the leather and metal headplate.

Jael's fingers slid over the pocked and pitted surface. "It also has many holes. And you think hailstones did this?"

"Hah!" Mathoni bellowed, startling Jael. "God stoned them to death with hailstones!"

"Oh, please, Mathoni!" Jael shoved the headplate back in his hands.

Jonas returned and said, "During the days of the prophet Joshua, God smote the land of Azekah with hailstones because they fought against the Israelites. The brass plates say that more people died from the hailstones than the children of Israel slew with the sword."

"Now I see more reason in staying on the Lord's side," said Mathoni in a more somber tone. He dropped the headplate back on the ground. "I am glad I was not one of the wicked who was slain. The further we go in this darkness, the more I realize how much the Lord has blessed us." He pulled Jael to his side, and she smiled at the growing peace she sensed within Mathoni.

"It will not be easy to get by this fallen battalion," Jonas said. "There are hundreds of men and weapons. We shall have to grope our way along the courtyard walls on the roadside."

A chill lingered within Jael as she flattened herself against wall after wall to get by. She stepped over headplates and shields meant to protect these men, and her feet often brushed their lifeless limbs. Her stomach clenched. She was glad to not have to view the horrid scene.

Even after they were long past the battalion, Jael felt sick. What a blessing to have Mathoni at her side to steady her. She gripped the edge of his deerskin vest for security and wished for a way to capture his endless strength to renew her weary body. For a moment she longed for him to carry her, as he had carried Mathonihah during their childhood.

"It must have been hard for Mathonihah to not run and play games with the other boys," she said.

"We had our share of games that required sitting in one place."

"And pranks," added Jonas. "Such as the nut trees."

"What nut trees?" asked Jael.

"The ones that grow along the highway, not far outside of the east gates of Bountiful," said Mathoni. "Nearly every day, Mathonihah begged us to help him climb into the broad branches. Then we would conceal ourselves in the thick leaves and drop nuts down on people traveling along the highway."

"We often were caught, and people demanded that we come down and be punished," said Jonas.

"But when we helped Mathonihah from the tree, and they saw his crippled foot, the scoldings never lasted long."

"Just think!" exclaimed Jonas. "In this darkness, we could drop nuts all day long and no one would ever catch us."

"We could get away with many things," agreed Mathoni, giving Jael a gentle squeeze.

She smiled and leaned her head against his arm. Warm thoughts drifted through her heart. Though her body became more weary with each precarious placing of her feet, she sensed their journey was drawing to an end.

Liahona's high-pitched whimper jolted Jael's weakened frame. Then another shock wave rippled the earth. "Oh, please, not again!" she moaned, clutching Mathoni with both hands.

"I might begin to enjoy earthquakes," he whispered in her ear. "But this is a mere tremor—nothing compared to the quaking when the darkness first began."

"Yet each tremor makes me more anxious about Mother." Jael again gripped Mathoni's vest as they stepped slowly onward. "How hard it is to sense that someone is suffering and not be able to help them for days and days!"

"Or years and years, which is how it is when God wants to

help His children here on earth. Suffering is just as difficult for Him to witness as it is for us to experience. Yet, as with all adversity, if we endure it well, there are promised rewards."

"After enduring the present darkness, the reward is the appearance of Jesus Christ?" asked Jael.

"There is a prophecy by Isaiah in the brass plates which foretells that glorious event: 'The people that walked in darkness have seen a great light; they that dwell in the land of the shadow of death, upon them hath the light shined.'"

"The land of the shadow of death," echoed Mathoni.

"Of course," said Jonas, "the great light Isaiah speaks of is Jesus Christ, the Light of the World."

"Will He show anger toward us when He comes?" Jael asked. "Or will He be kind?"

"Have we not already witnessed the depths of His anger?" asked Mathoni.

"Yes," answered Jonas. "When He appears, I believe He will restore peace and love in the land. Our forefather Nephi prophesied this of Christ's appearance: 'The Son of righteousness shall appear unto them, and he shall heal them, and they shall have peace with him.'"

"He shall heal them," said Jael. "It sounds as if Jesus may teach you something about healing people, Mathoni."

"I am certain I have much to learn."

Jael stepped through a small puddle, and mud oozed between her toes. She wanted to stop and shake out the mud, but Mathoni seemed to increase his pace. "Is something amiss?" she asked.

"Can you not hear it?" Mathoni's voice was tense. "There are people crying out for help again. We are not alone in this part of the land Bountiful."

THIRTEEN

Jael strained to hear. "They are yet far off."

"Close or far. How can I ignore them?"

"The Lord is mindful of their needs," said Jonas. "He will send someone to help them."

"Do you not believe I am that someone?"

Jonas tapped steadily forward with Liahona panting nearby. "You and your father are not the only physicians in the land Bountiful."

Jael let Mathoni help her across a small crevice. This journey through the perils and darkness was the most difficult task she had ever faced. With each questionable step along the rugged road she felt more grateful for Mathoni's comforting presence. Perhaps Jonas would tell her to be grateful for the presence and comfort of the Holy Spirit. But her heart was too burdened and her body too weary to truly understand that now.

Nearing the voices in the darkness, Jael tugged on Mathoni's vest. "Listen. The people are not crying for help but praying for forgiveness."

"Perhaps you are right."

"Yes," agreed Jonas, "it sounds as though they are holding a worship service."

Moments later, the voices broke into song: "May the Lord preserve his people in righteousness. May the Lord preserve his people in holiness. Hosanna! Blessed be the name of the Most High God. Hosanna! Blessed be the name of the Almighty God."

"It is just as I said. They are holding a worship service." Jonas moved ahead more rapidly. "While they are assembled I shall deliver Father's message to them."

Lagging behind Jonas, Liahona bumped up against Jael's legs. She reached down and patted his head.

"Is this another synagogue?" Mathoni asked.

"I know of no synagogue here." Jonas tapped the stick to their right. "These people are out in the open somewhere, and there are hundreds of voices, which means many were spared in this part of the land."

"What faith they must have to worship and praise the Lord in this darkness," said Mathoni.

Jael smiled, realizing that he was making a greater effort to let his own faith grow. As the singing ended, she heard the faint words of a man praying.

Jonas waited until the prayer was over before tapping his stick again toward the congregation. "I believe there is a burial ground in this location."

"A perfect place to assemble in the land of the shadow of death," mused Mathoni.

"Perhaps they are burying their dead," said Jael. Then she listened to the chatter of their voices—inquiring after each other's welfare.

Before their babble rose, Jonas called to them through the darkness. "Brethren and sisters, please listen. I have a word to say unto you from the Prophet Nephi. I know you cannot see me, but I am Jonas, son of Nephi. Perhaps you recall when I came here with him to preach the gospel?"

Jonas paused for their affirmation.

"Go on, Brother Jonas," called a man from within the group. "Tell us the words of Nephi."

"He would have us all assemble at the temple. There is a need to take an accounting of those who remain alive."

An uproar began with voices concerned about traveling through the darkness and destruction.

"Please! Please listen!" Jonas' voice resounded. The voices

softened, though a murmur continued, and Jonas had to shout to be heard. "I have traveled in this darkness from my father's house to deliver his message to you. You must come to the temple because that is where the Lord Jesus Christ will appear when the light returns."

A hush fell over the crowd. Jonas lowered his voice. "Many prophets have said that, after these days of darkness, Jesus Christ will come to visit this land."

"At the first dawning of light?" someone asked.

"When He feels our hearts and minds are ready to receive Him," Jonas said in a solemn tone. "Because there has been much destruction upon the face of the land, I suggest you wait until the darkness fades, then gather some provisions and come with your families to the temple."

"Brother Jonas," called a man from the midst of the crowd. "Please, abide a while that I may speak further with you."

"Who are you?" asked Jonas.

"Lemhiah, one of the judges in this part of the land." His voice neared. "Please, let me through so I may speak to the son of Nephi." Feet shuffled as people parted to let the man through. "Thank you for waiting, Jonas." Lemhiah came forward, sucking in deep breaths from his excitement. "Your father's brother, Timothy, was here a short while after the darkness began. He told us nothing about journeying to the temple."

Once again the congregation began to prattle, causing Jonas to raise his voice. "Uncle Timothy does not know. I am on my way to tell him."

Lemhiah stood so close to Jael that she felt his hot breath on her face when he spoke. "Surely you are not traveling alone through this darkness."

"I have come with my cousin, Jael, and my friend, Mathoni, son of Zedekiah the physician."

"Did you have to tell them?" Mathoni said in a hushed but

gruff tone. "Now we may be stuck here tending to the wounded."

"You have no need for concern," Jonas said quietly to his friend. "I believe these people are so righteous that they have come through the tempests and the quakes with little damage."

"How can you know in this blackness?" asked Mathoni.

Jael snuggled closer to Mathoni to get away from Lemhiah's portly stomach, pressing against her. "Why do you not ask Lemhiah?" she whispered. "Then you shall know whether or not they have wounded who need your medical skills."

"Only a few here were wounded," Lemhiah said, overhearing their conversation. "And they have received good care from Nahab, a physician who lives nearby."

"The Lord has been merciful to us," said a woman.

"Praise the Lord," responded another. "Hosanna! Blessed be the name of the Most High God."

The people spontaneously began to sing again. "Hosanna! Blessed be the name of the Almighty God."

"Tell your father we shall come to the temple," Lemhiah said over the hymning.

"You may see him before I do. We have many other people to visit before journeying back to the temple." Jonas turned to his companions. "We have delivered our message. We are free to go." Jael and Mathoni followed his tapping stick back to the highway while Liahona yapped at their heels. Then Jonas began to hum the hymn the people had sung.

"You seem happy," Jael said to him.

"I am indeed! We are nearing the end of our journey. Uncle Timothy's house cannot be far off, and the river is just beyond."

Mathoni's arm tensed across Jael's back. She slipped her arm around his waist. He must still be worried about his sister. "How far is it to Martha's house?"

"From your house, it is a fair distance downstream. In this darkness, it may take a few hours to get there."

Her fingers pressed into his side. How could she ever let him go? She may never find him again.

"After I see to Martha's family, I shall come back to get you at your house. Then we shall travel together to the temple."

"Do you believe we will see Jesus Christ there?"

"This incredible darkness has made me believe many things I never thought I would."

Yes, the darkness was incredible. Jael swiped at it as if to get a handful. For hours and days the heavy vapor had shrouded the world. She would be glad when it finally faded away. "Jonas, do the plates tell of other times when darkness and destruction came upon the earth?"

"One of the plagues Moses brought upon Egypt was a curse of three days of darkness, followed by other destructive plagues." Jonas rapped the stick and moved slowly forward. "There was also great destruction at the time of Noah when the Lord destroyed the wicked with a flood, though there was no darkness at that time."

"It was a dark time for the wicked," said Mathoni. "I would prefer three days of darkness to drowning in a flood."

"And I would prefer to have my world back the way it used to be." Jael tried to picture the scene around her—the highway, the homes, the people with whom she had been familiar. Now many were dead and others were left weeping and mourning. And what of Mother? Weak, fevered, racked by fits of coughing. A long time had passed since the tempest and earthquakes began. Was Mother still alive? Jael bowed her head. A shudder rolled down her back.

"Are you all right?" Mathoni asked. She leaned her head against his arm and nodded. Her legs seemed heavier now as they worked their way along. Mathoni tipped his head against hers. "It has been a long journey through the mists of darkness to reach your home."

"Yet the Lord has blessed us to travel in safety," said Jonas.

"He has promised that the righteous need not fear. Jael, you asked if the plates told of other times when darkness and destruction came upon the earth. Both the brass plates and the plates of Nephi contain prophecies of what are called the latter days, foretelling of fires, tempests, and earthquakes rending the earth. Also at that time, the sun and moon will be darkened."

"And Jesus Christ shall come again to visit the earth," added Mathoni.

"Yes, that is also prophesied," said Jonas. "How did you know?"

"I have not forgotten all the scriptures I learned in my youth. Your father often preached from the pulpit what would occur during the last days upon the earth."

"In those days, Jesus Christ shall do more than just visit his people. He will actually come to dwell upon the earth and reign with power and great glory." Jonas' voice sounded energetic. "Can you imagine what righteousness and peace will abound in the world then?"

Jael tried to imagine a world without Lamanite wars or Gadianton robbers, a world without anger or fear, a world without sorrow. What a blessed time!

The strap of her sandal snagged on something. She grabbed Mathoni with both hands to keep from falling. "Forgive me. I failed to concentrate on my walking."

"I would rather have you concentrate on me." Mathoni drew her closer. The satchel slid off his shoulder and bumped against her thigh, but she barely noticed. His muscled arms pulled her tightly against his chest.

Jael took in a quivering breath. She sensed Mathoni had lowered his face near hers and wondered if he might kiss her. Then she no longer had to wonder. He lightly touched his lips on her forehead, her cheek, and her mouth.

Their fragile moment hung suspended in the dark mist, while Jonas continued forward without them. But Liahona soon spoiled their interlude by barking a warning to Jonas. "What is it, Liahona? What are you telling me?"

Through the haze of her bliss, Jael heard the dog chasing back towards them. His wide front paws bounced against her legs.

"Away with you, Liahona!" Mathoni bent slightly to push the dog down. "I know you are jealous, but I shall not share Jael with you, not for one second. We were companions in this darkness before you came along."

"Mathoni, Jael, where are you?" Jonas called.

"Here." Mathoni gave her forehead a final kiss and again anchored his arm at her waist. "We had better move on."

"No," said Jael, her voice barely a whisper. "I think my sandal is broken."

Jonas huffed up beside her. "Are you hurt?"

"I . . . I," Jael's mouth would not work.

"Her sandal may have broken," Mathoni said for her.

Still trembling from the thrill of Mathoni's embrace, Jael leaned down to feel the sandal. The strap across her toes was missing.

"Jael?" Jonas questioned.

"The strap is gone," she sighed. "And now I fear I will slow our journey all the more."

"I will see what I can do," announced Mathoni. His hands found her knees. Then his fingers slid slowly, ever so slowly, toward her feet. Her diaphragm spasmed. Goose bumps sprouted from her feet to her neck. She crossed her arms and tried to rub the flesh smooth. But it was hopeless as long as Mathoni's hands remained upon her ankle and foot.

"I have an idea." He let go momentarily.

Jael tried to clear her head, relieved that the darkness hid her face from Jonas.

"Lift up your foot," said Mathoni after a moment. Then he again grasped her ankle, and she took in a sharp breath.

"Jael?" asked Jonas. "Are you all right?"

She did not know what to say.

A soft chuckle came from Mathoni's throat. "She is fine. I shall try to give her a little support by tying my headband around the sandal where the strap used to be."

Jael tried to breathe evenly and ignore the wild emotions erupting inside her.

"There you go," Mathoni said, standing.

Jael thought, yes, there I go. I have gone over the brink of a cliff, and I am floating through the air with no fear of falling.

"Jael?" Jonas' voice finally called her back to a firm landing. "Are you ready to move on?"

"Yes," she said softly.

Mathoni's arm found her waist. "I believe the sandal will hold together long enough for you to get home."

Liahona barked as they once again made their way through the black vapor. Jael found it difficult to walk with the mended sandal. Often her foot slipped sideways, and soon it began to ache. The further they passed through the dark corridors, the more painful her foot became.

"Something is about to happen!" Jonas said suddenly. "I can feel it!"

"I have felt that way for two days," said Mathoni.

"I hear voices again," Jonas said as he quickly moved ahead. Jael heard the uneven thud of his feet as he stumbled across the dark terrain. Then her cousin's voice shouted, "Uncle Timothy? Is that you, Uncle Timothy?"

FOURTEEN

"How can it be Uncle Timothy?" Jael asked Mathoni. "His home is close enough to the river to hear the water."

"If it is Timothy, he will have word of your mother and others in this quarter of the land." Mathoni's fingers dug more deeply into her side as he urged her along. The broken sandal barely held together as they fumbled their way across the uneven ground.

"Uncle Timothy!" Jonas shouted again.

"Is someone there?" a voice called back.

"Yes. Jonas, son of Nephi."

"It is a spirit!" said another voice.

"No. I am here in the flesh. I have come to bring you a message from my father. Is my uncle with you?"

"Yes, Jonas!" Uncle Timothy's voice was filled with excitement. "You have a message from Nephi? What a welcome blessing on this dark day!"

As she neared, Jael pictured the two men embracing and heard the chatter of their voices.

"What? Jael is with you, also?" Uncle Timothy asked. "It is a miracle that you have found your way here."

"The Lord has been merciful," Jonas replied. "We had some help from a stray dog. Also from my friend Mathoni."

Jael gave Mathoni's ribs a squeeze. "He is comparing you to a stray dog." She expected laughter, but he failed to respond.

He remained silent until they reached Jonas' side. "Hail, Timothy and brethren, from Mathoni, son of Zedekiah the physician." After the men greeted him, he said, "Jael is concerned for her mother's welfare. Have you word of her?"

"Jael, come here." Uncle Timothy's groping hands found her shoulders, and he embraced her. "After the storm, I went first to your mother's house. Though Esther is frail and of ill health, she came through the tempest and earthquakes better than many of her neighbors. But she feared for you and Seth. She shall be pleased to have you return home."

"Praise the Lord!" said Jael. "I cannot wait to see her!"

"It may be a while before you actually see her," said Jonas. "We are not yet through with the three days of darkness."

"I hope we are nearing the final hours," said Timothy.

Jonas' voice sounded hesitant. "Perhaps we should pray for release from the darkness."

"We have prayed for the injured and administered blessings to many," said Timothy, "but such a prayer is a worthy suggestion. Is that the message Nephi asked you to deliver?"

"No, Uncle Timothy. Do you recall the prophecies that Jesus Christ will visit this land after the darkness fades?"

"Yes, and will He come immediately when the light returns?"

"Perhaps not. But when the darkness disperses, Father has asked that we assemble at the temple to make an accounting of those who remain alive. And to await the coming of the Lord."

"Would he have me gather people from this part of the land?"

"Yes. Are you on your way somewhere?"

"Brother Helorum just told us of a family downriver who needs assistance. We were on our way there, but we first need to secure the help of Nahab, the physician. Now that your friend Mathoni has joined us, perhaps we can take him with us instead."

"I would be honored to join you," said Mathoni. "But my first duty, outlined by our noble prophet Nephi, is to escort his niece safely home."

"That is upriver and out of the way," someone said.

"I know, Helorum," answered Timothy.

"Tell me where you are going," said Mathoni, "and I shall join you as soon as I am able."

"To the home of Jeremiah and Leah. They have a large farm, which their children and grandchildren help to cultivate. It is said that a storehouse collapsed, and many are trapped."

"Because they are not near other farms," Helorum's voice broke in, "it has taken a while for word to reach us. Perhaps even now it is too late to save them, but we must go and try."

"Your medical skills will be needed, Mathoni," said Timothy. "After taking Jael home, could you find your way to the farm of Jeremiah and Leah?"

"I know the way well," Mathoni said with a tremor in his voice. "Jeremiah and Leah are the parents of my sister's husband. Martha and her family reside at that farm."

"Oh, Mathoni!" Jael reached up to place her hands on his shoulders. He seemed limp with despair.

He drew her into an embrace, though his arms lacked their usual vigor. "I was forewarned by the Spirit that Martha needed my help. Surely, the Lord is mindful of her, and I must have faith that He will grant a special blessing in her behalf."

Jael pressed her cheek against his deerskin vest and felt the thunder of his strong heart. Though she longed to remain close beside him and continue to rely on his strength, she said, "Mathoni, you must go to Martha's aid."

"And what of your mother?"

"I shall go to her. It is not far, and I know my way well through this part of the land."

"The land has changed with the earthquakes," said Jonas.

"Perhaps you would go with her?" Mathoni asked his friend.

"Or one of the other brethren?" suggested Uncle Timothy.

"Thank you, but I shall not need to be accompanied. There are others in need. Please take care of them." As she spoke, she had to swallow away the fear that hardened in her throat.

Though the darkness was a tangible threat, the thought of not seeing Mathoni again was what choked her.

"I shall come to your mother's house as soon as I am able," Mathoni assured her. "Would you like to take my stick with you?"

"Only as a memory of you," she said softly. "It failed to help me when I was in trouble before."

"Then you must take Liahona," Jonas said firmly. "He will warn you of dangers along the way."

"Yes. I would prefer a dog to a stick as a traveling companion," she said, trying to sound light-hearted.

"I shall offer a prayer of safety before we separate," said Uncle Timothy. "And, as Jonas has suggested, we shall also pray for this darkness to soon disperse." He turned to hush some of the brethren, who then gathered quietly.

Jael bowed her head. Beneath her folded arms, her heartbeat gradually decreased as Uncle Timothy's words rose heavenward. Within her soul she prayed that Mathoni would soon be reunited with her. When the prayer ended, Jael leaned against him.

"Are you certain you can find your way?" he asked.

Jael nodded against his chest, and for a final moment she lingered with the warmth of his arms across her back.

"The Spirit of the Lord will guide you home through the mists of darkness," he said, "as Jonas has often reminded us."

"Thank you, Jonas." Jael hugged her cousin.

"My sash is around Liahona's neck." Jonas gave the end to her. "So he should stay at your side."

Mathoni handed her the bedroll. "You may need this for warmth." His lips brushed her cheek.

"Oh, please, Mathoni. Just go." She shut her eyes against the welling tears. "I shall abide here with Liahona and rest." A sob clogged her throat. Why did it hurt so much to say goodbye to Mathoni? Two days ago she was not even sure she liked him.

"We will go to the temple together," he said.

"Yes." Jael stood as erect as possible while the men departed. Then she set the bedroll on the ground, sat on it, and pulled Liahona's head onto her lap. She took in a deep breath and thought about her homeland. This was where she belonged, where she had been coddled by loving parents, safeguarded by neighbors, and cherished by friends. She should feel more secure here than anywhere else.

With quivering hands, she stroked Liahona's fur, while the taunting black vapor crawled around her shoulders. Now her safe world had changed—how much she did not know. And never before had she felt so all alone.

FIFTEEN

Jael sighed and scratched Liahona behind the ears. "At least I still have you." Tears rolled from her eyes and spilled into his fur. Liahona raised up and began to lick the moisture from her cheeks. "Oh, please, Liahona." She could not keep herself from grinning. "Is this your way of telling me to move on? Or is it that my face needs washing? How nice it shall be to soak for a while in the river!" She stood and brushed the dirt from her borrowed dress. "And how nice it shall be to put on a dress that fits." Taking the bedroll in one hand, she wrapped the end of the sash-made-into-leash around her other hand. Liahona barked in anticipation.

"I wonder what Mother will think of me bringing home a dog. Because of her midwifing, she never allowed us to have pets—not even a lamb or chickens as some of our friends had."

Liahona tugged eagerly on the leash, while Jael slid one foot then the next along the crusted highway. She had to trust the dog to warn her if dangers materialized in the darkness. Occasional voices cried out and startled her, but no one actually crossed her path. Liahona seemed content, sniffing the air and barking as new smells or sounds arose around them. Often the broken sandal caught on bushes or rubble along the way. When she stopped to readjust the headband tied around the sandal, a longing for Mathoni swelled within her. How she missed him— his breadth, his height, his warmth!

She also missed her cousin's spiritual gifts. But as time wore on, she gained confidence in her own ability to heed the whisperings of the Spirit. As Jonas had assured her, there truly was a Presence to comfort and guide her. Peace filled her soul, and her heart soared like a bird with a newly-healed wing. She realized, as never before, that the Lord was mindful of her on this dark journey homeward.

Still, the hours dragged by and she seemed to make little progress. Her stomach rumbled with hunger. Her legs ached with fatigue. She nearly abandoned the bedroll, for it seemed too much of a burden. Then she remembered it belonged to Mathoni, and she hugged it tightly to her breast.

Finally she heard the distant babble of the river. Liahona stopped abruptly and she nearly stumbled over him. A deep growl arose in his throat. Jael knelt and wrapped her arms around his neck—partly to restrain him, but more for something to hold onto. "What is it, Liahona? What do you sense?" Liahona barked so sharply that Jael's ears rang. "Hush, now!" she commanded and tapped her fingers on his snout. He stilled, though his body jerked and twitched with mounting tension. Then Jael heard soft footsteps and someone weeping. "Hello?" she called into the blackness. "Is someone there?"

The footsteps ceased. Liahona's throat rumbled again.

"Is someone there?" Jael asked once more.

"Y-y-yes," came a quivering child's voice.

"It is all right," Jael soothed. "You have nothing to fear."

"Who are you?"

"My name is Jael. I live near the river with my mother and younger brother. What is your name?"

"Sarah."

"Hush, Liahona." Again Jael rapped his nose to quiet his growling. "How old are you, Sarah?"

"Eleven."

"How is it that you are here in this darkness alone?"

"I . . . I," the child choked on her tears.

Jael secured her grasp on Liahona and gradually stepped forward. "I have a dog with me. His name is Liahona. You have no fear of dogs, do you?"

"No," came a muffled response, as if the girl's face were buried in her hands.

Jael reached out and found Sarah sitting on the ground with her head bowed against her knees. "Are you all right? Were you hurt in the tempest and earthquakes?"

"No." Sarah spoke through her tears. "But my parents both died when our roof fell in."

"I am so sorry about your parents. Would that they might have lived." Jael sat down on her bedroll and tucked an arm around Sarah's shoulders. "Is there someone who could look after you now? A relative or friend who lives nearby?"

Sarah's head slumped against Jael's chest and her tears moistened the borrowed dress. "My brother. He is married now. I was trying to find my way to his house."

"Where does he live?"

Sarah sniffled. "By the river, near the big tree that you can swing from."

Jael released a tense breath of air. "I, too, live near that tree. I am on my way there now. Would you like to come with me? I shall try to help you find your brother." Sarah's head nodded against Jael's chest. "Have you been by yourself since the darkness began?"

"I stayed with my parents for a long time. I kept hoping one of them might wake up." She paused and sniffled again. "I waited and waited. But neither of them moved. Then somehow I knew they were dead and I had to find my brother."

"You are brave to venture out in this darkness alone."

Sarah shook her head. "I am fearful. What if my brother . . . what if he is also dead?"

Jael's heart wrenched. And what of Mother? She waited for the pang within her to subside, then said, "Let us pray that your brother is alive and well. But if not, you may come to live with our family. I have often longed for a sister."

"As have I." Sarah wrapped her arms around Jael's neck.

"Thank you. I am not as fearful now that you are with me."

"I can hear the river. It should not take long to find our way to my house." Jael stood and gathered her belongings.

"Do you have food at your house? I am very hungry."

"We had a good supply when I left home a few days ago." Jael draped an arm across Sarah's shoulders and began to guide her along.

Liahona strained at his leash on their way to the gushing river. They found the banks were muddy and cluttered with debris. Jael let go of Liahona's leash and tried to push the rubble aside to clear the way. Though she had often seen the river rise after a storm, never had it collected such trash. She felt her way through broken furniture, rotting logs, leather halters, wagon wheels, and other shattered items that had caught in bushes on the riverbank.

Jael could no longer guide Sarah with an arm across her shoulders. "Hold my dress with one hand," she suggested, "and stay directly behind me." Jael's feet, raw from days of traveling, stung with open wounds as she clambered over obstacles along the bank. She felt relief each time cool water from the river splashed on her wounds.

"Where did Liahona go?" Sarah asked as Jael helped her scramble over a pile of timbers.

"A little way ahead." Jael freed her dress from a jagged piece of wood. "What kind of work does your brother do?"

"He makes wagons. He used to be just an apprentice. Then he got married, about a year ago, and began to make his own wagons to sell."

"Is his name Micah?"

"Yes! Do you know him?"

"His house is near mine. I have seen him building wagons in the shop behind his house."

"His wife's name is Hava."

"I also know Hava. She is soon due to have a baby."

"I like to visit Micah and Hava so I can swing from the cord tied in the big tree. Have you ever tried it?"

"Yes." Jael smiled at the memory. For a moment she wished to be a carefree child again, even if it meant making a fool of herself in front of Mathoni. "I think we are nearing that old tree now. It should be just beyond this bend in the river."

"I hope so. My legs are tired."

"My legs are also weary. I have been walking for a long while." Jael clawed her way through a bushy willow, then paused. "Sarah, wait here for a moment while I search the darkness."

Jael groped forward. She longed to part the black mist and see the broad tree, the landmark to assure that she was nearly home. Soon her sweeping hands brushed rough wood, but it was not what she expected—not limbs, but roots—ripped from the storm-torn riverbank. She shook her head and pictured the enormous tree, broken and sprawled on the bank—never again to swing a child from its branches.

"Jael?" Sarah called. "Where are you?"

"I am coming back toward you now. I found the tree with the swing, but it has fallen. We shall have to wade into the river and hold onto the roots as we go by."

"What about Liahona?"

"He will have to swim." Jael shifted the bedroll strap to her other shoulder and took Sarah by one hand. "Go in front of me and grasp the tree roots as you wade into the water. The current is swift, but I shall stay behind to help you." Jael directed the girl's hands toward the roots, and together they stepped off the bank and into the river.

Sarah caught her breath. "It is cold."

"And deeper than usual." The broken sandal pulled heavily in the water, and Jael hoped she would not lose it. The river came nearly to her hips, making each stride a major effort.

Sarah toiled forward, inches at a time, with Jael's hand on

one shoulder to steady her. Then Sarah lost her grip and screamed. Her body slammed into Jael. The blow dazed Jael and knocked the wind from her lungs. As she gasped for air, the bedroll slid off her shoulder and was gone. Jael struggled to hold Sarah under one arm while the current tried to drag them both downstream.

"I am slipping!" Sarah shrieked.

Jael anchored her feet in the muddy river bottom. She hooked an arm around Sarah's chest and pulled her upward. Sarah's hand found its way to Jael's neck. Jael winced as the girl's nails clawed into her flesh. Then a sudden wave hit them. Jael choked and fought to hang onto Sarah. She twisted her body toward the bank. "Sarah! Try to grab the roots again!"

Sarah's arms flailed. Water sloshed in Jael's face. "I have it," Sarah said weakly.

Jael kept one hand anchored under Sarah's arm. "Can you make it?"

"I shall try." Once again Sarah inched her way forward.

"You are almost there. Keep holding the roots until you are out of danger." The water line moved from mid-thigh to her knees. She waded into a pool which the fallen tree must have formed. "Praise the Lord! We made it!" Jael hugged Sarah.

Liahona yapped and leaped upon them. Jael patted his wet fur. Then she took off Rebekah's shawl and handed it to Sarah. "Hold this for a moment." With a shudder of joy, Jael sank into the pool of water.

"What are you doing?" Sarah asked.

"Washing away the dirt and grime from my journey." Jael stretched back her neck and let the chilly water swirl around her head. She massaged her scalp, raked her fingers through the tangled locks of hair, then splashed water on her face. Had the river been warmer, she would have stayed longer.

A renewed vigor lifted her to her feet. Alongside Sarah, she waded to the shore, where she wrung out her dress and shook the moisture from her hair. Then she again wrapped the shawl around her shoulders. Liahona braced his paws against her thigh. She reached for the leash at his neck and discovered it was gone--washed downriver with Mathoni's bedroll. Her brow furrowed and she wondered if Mathoni was all right.

Sarah groped for Jael's hand. "Can we find my brother now?"

Jael took in a quivering breath. "I must first make sure my mother is all right. She is ill and has been alone since the tempest began."

"Will she have a fire to warm us and dry our clothes?"

"Only if she has worked a miracle." Jael began to lead Sarah up the embankment, yet the bulky branches of the fallen tree fought against them. "We shall have to go further upstream."

"But that will take us away from my brother's house."

"We shall find our way back. I know all the houses along this stretch of river." Jael led Sarah along the river's edge until she located a place to scramble up the slanted bank with Liahona at their heels. Then Jael stopped to catch her breath. "Did you hear that?"

"What?" asked Sarah.

"A woman weeping, perhaps? I am not sure. I may have imagined it."

"After the earthquakes, many people were weeping."

"Yes, I also heard them." Jael tucked an arm across Sarah's shoulders. Her other arm groped through the darkness as they made their way toward the houses. "Now is when I wish I had Mathoni's stick."

"Is Mathoni your husband?"

Jael laughed. "I am not yet married. He is but a friend."

"You seem old enough to be married."

"Perhaps." Until now, marriage to Mathoni had not crossed her mind. Memories of him drifted through her like rose petals on a breeze. Her shoulders lifted and she smiled.

"Ow!" Sarah moaned.

"What is it?"

"A twig with thorns. It scratched my leg."

"Forgive me for not being a better leader," Jael said, then added with a grin, "You should watch where you are going."

Sarah giggled. "I wish I could."

A short while later, Jael's hand contacted a wall of mud bricks. She ran her fingers along it until she touched a bush. Though most of the leaves and blossoms had been shattered by the tempest, she recognized the lingering smell. "Lilacs," she said softly. "This is the home of Gideon, who supplies our village with oil lamps."

"We could use an oil lamp now," said Sarah.

"Yes, we could." Jael followed the wall to the corner then up the side yard to the front of the house. Her heart beat faster in anticipation. "The home of Benjamin the tanner is next, and then mine."

"And my brother's house?"

"Two beyond mine."

"Could we pretend to be sisters even if Micah is alive?"

"It would be a pleasure to have a sister such as you." Jael led Sarah past Benjamin's house.

Then, in the darkness, a woman wailed in agony. The cry came from within the walls of Jael's home.

SIXTEEN

Jael thrust Sarah in the direction of the wailing. They met with the mud brick wall and felt their way to the door. With shaky hands, Jael grasped the latch and shoved it open. The door scraped against the dirt floor. "Mother? Mother, it is I, Jael! Do you need help?"

"Jael! Praise the Lord!" Esther's weak voice came from the farthest corner of the room.

Jael rubbed her hands up and down her chilled arms. "Are you all right, Mother? I heard someone cry out in pain."

"The cry was not mine but Hava's, who is in travail. Micah is here with her."

"Micah!" Sarah called. "Micah, where are you?"

"Sarah?" His voice came closer. "How did you find your way through the darkness?"

"Jael helped me." Sarah let go of Jael and moved toward her brother. Instantly she began to sob. "Oh, Micah! Mother and Father both died in the earthquake."

Liahona barked, and Jael tapped his nose to quiet him.

"Jael, I do not understand . . ." Esther began to cough.

Jael stepped slowly forward. "I found Micah's sister alone in the darkness and brought her home with me. Also a stray dog."

Esther's coughing eased. "And what of your brother, Seth?"

"He stayed with Uncle Nephi." Jael's eager hands found Mother's chair beside the birthing bed. She knelt and put one arm around the frail shoulders. "Oh, Mother! How I have worried for you as I traveled in the darkness!"

"As I worried for you." Mother stroked Jael's hair with one hand. "You are wet and chilled. What a journey you must have had through the darkness."

"Jonas and his friend Mathoni helped me find my way until a short time ago. Then they left with Uncle Timothy to go help Mathoni's sister and her family."

"What a blessing to have you here, Jael. I am far too weary to midwife with Hava."

"How can a child be born in this darkness?"

"I have never known a woman to choose when her child is to be born."

Jael stood behind the chair and placed her hands on Mother's shoulders. "I shall be honored to help with the birth."

"Helping is not enough. You shall have to be the midwife. My right wrist is broken and useless."

"No! Uncle Timothy said you were all right."

"An old woman's bones break easily. In this darkness it was easy to conceal my arm from Timothy. I asked him to give me a blessing then sent him on his way to help others in need."

Hava began to moan. Esther leaned forward. "Here, Hava, you may bite on this cloth during the pain."

Sarah came to Jael's side. "Will Hava be all right?"

"Yes." Jael patted Sarah's shoulder. "She is young and strong. And Mother is an excellent midwife."

Hava's moaning increased, and she thrashed against the bed-straw. Micah brushed by Jael and knelt at the bedside. "Why must there be so much pain?"

"The first child is often more difficult. It may be a long while before we see the rewards of Hava's labor." Esther coughed for a moment, then added, "The house of birth is no place for a worried husband. Before Jael arrived, I needed your help, Micah. Now it is better that you take your sister and go home. I shall send Jael to get you after the child is born."

The moaning ceased, and Hava made an effort to speak, "Micah, do as Esther has said. I shall bring a fine child into the world for you."

"I love you, Hava," Micah said, then he came to stand on the other side of Sarah.

"Do you have food at your house?" Sarah asked. "I have not eaten for a long while."

"We have a good supply. Hava has been preparing for the day of her travail."

"Sarah also needs some dry clothing," said Jael.

Sarah touched Jael's arm. "Can we pretend to be sisters?"

"Certainly." Jael hugged the girl. "Now, off with you. Mother and I have work to do. But you can help by taking Liahona with you when you go."

"Yes, I shall." Sarah walked across the room with Micah. "Come, Liahona."

Jael heard the dog follow them out the door. Then the room was quiet except for Hava's tense breathing.

Esther reached up to pat Jael's hand. "You must find something dry to wear."

A smile lit Jael's weary countenance. Finally she could undress without Mathoni hovering nearby. She unwrapped Rebekah's shawl then tugged the borrowed dress over her head. "At least I am clean after my journey."

"A midwife does well to serve with clean hands."

Carrying the wet clothing across the room, Jael laid them out to dry on chairs beside the table. The aroma of something made her stomach growl. She patted her hands along the table to see what she might find. Honeycomb. The honey stuck to her fingers and she licked it off. "Mother, is there any bread?"

"Yes, the loaves you made before leaving for Nephi's are on the table," Esther said in a feeble tone.

Hava's moans again filled the dark air. Jael ate the bread and honey quickly, then went to a wooden box for some dry clothes.

Esther spoke gently to Hava. "You must again lift your skirts so I can check the progress you are making."

After a moment, Esther began to cough. Jael finished

dressing and groped her way across the room. "Oh, please, Mother! Your cough sounds worse. You must go to bed and rest. I shall tend to Hava until the birth draws nearer."

"My cough is no better or worse than when it started months ago. But my wrist is aching. And I know I can trust you to do what is necessary."

Jael eased Mother off the chair, led her to the adjacent room, and tucked her into bed.

"The vigil at Hava's bedside may be long and difficult." Mother patted Jael's arm. "She is not a large woman, and I have midwifed at the bedside of her sisters. Jael, you have learned the skills of midwifing well. Even in the darkness, your hands will know what to do."

Jael shivered as fear washed through her. She longed to believe in the skills she had been taught, but never had she midwifed without Mother's help. And in the darkness besides! From the next room, Hava groaned again. Jael folded her taut hands together and searched within for courage. "Sleep well," she sighed and kissed Mother's cheek.

Then she groped her way to the birthing bed. "Hava, I shall sponge your forehead to help you relax." Beside the bed, she found a basin of water and a soft cloth. The water was not warm, as she was used to using, but with no fire she had little choice. Jael wrung out the cloth, swabbed Hava's forehead, then her arms and hands. "You must not fight against the pains. Let your body do what it must to bring this baby forth."

Hava's groans ceased. She took in a quivering breath, and said weakly, "Your mother said the same thing moments before you came home. You are so much like her, Jael. Kind and caring. You shall make someone a fine wife."

Jael smiled. It was the second mention of marriage today. Her heartbeat quickened as she recalled the many hours spent at Mathoni's side. In the fervor of concern for him, her hand clenched the damp cloth, which dripped moisture onto her lap.

"I am glad you came," said Hava—her voice growing stronger. "I was worried about being a burden on your mother."

Jael set the cloth down. "Mother has been ill for several months. But there has never been a better midwife in this part of the land."

"Perhaps you shall be the one to follow in her stead."

"It would take a lifetime to master her skills."

"You are starting at a young age. You will have plenty of time to learn."

"All this talk is keeping you from resting, Hava. You must try to sleep between the pains. You will need all your strength to bring the baby forth."

"My throat is dry. Might I trouble you for a drink?"

"Surely." As Jael rose, she remembered the special wine Mother saved for such occasions. Yet she was not sure where to find it. "Did Mother already offer you some medicinal wine?"

"She offered it, but Micah would not allow me to drink any while he was here."

Jael shook her head. "What does he know? He has never been in travail. The wine will help you to relax. Perhaps then you shall be able to sleep." After searching the table with no success, she went toward the hook behind the door and found two flasks. She uncorked one and smelled the fruity tang of the fresh wine. She took a sip, and the juice soothed her own dry throat. She rehung that flask on the hook and carried the medicinal wine toward Hava. "Here. I shall help you raise up to take a drink." Jael slid a hand behind the woman's shoulders and gently lifted.

Hava held the flask to her lips, swallowed several times, then lay back upon the straw bed. "I shall try to sleep now."

"I will stay here beside you." Jael took the flask from Hava. She twisted the leather strap around the fingers of one hand. Then she untwisted the strap and leaned her head against the back of the chair. So much had happened in the last few days.

The memories strung through her mind like silken threads, intertwined in the darkness, with no beginning and no end. The only clear image was of Mathoni. She saw him as he had stood at Uncle Nephi's hearth with his muscled arms toting a stack of wood. She envisioned the glimmer of his teeth when he smiled and his left eyebrow rising when he first looked at her. Then she recalled the vain lift to his chin, which she had at first disliked. Now she realized that his self-assurance was what had helped pull her through the long, dark hours of her journey home.

When Hava's breathing became shallow and regular, Jael closed her eyes. How useless those eyes had been for days! She wondered what it would be like to finally see again. And more than anything, she longed for the sight of Mathoni.

Hava cried out in her sleep. Jael leaned forward and took the woman's hand. "Do not fear. I am still here beside you." Hava squeezed Jael's fingers until she felt they might break. Jael clenched her jaw against the pain and tried to pry her hand free. Now she knew she was too young to be a midwife. She had no idea what Hava was experiencing. She could only repeat the words her mother often said: "Oh, please, Hava! Do not fight against the pain, but let it flow through you."

Hava finally quit writhing and relaxed enough for Jael to pull her hand free. Then Jael dipped her throbbing fingers into the basin of cool water to soothe their aching. After a moment, she wrung out the cloth and began to sponge Hava's forehead. "Try to sleep once more," she suggested and set aside the cloth.

"My back hurts," Hava moaned. "Is it possible for me to turn on my side, facing you?"

"Certainly. Let me help you." Jael stretched past Hava's swollen abdomen and anchored both hands underneath her. "Now bend your knees and turn this way."

Jael's arms strained to pull Hava onto her side. Though the woman groaned, together they finally accomplished the task.

Then Hava managed a weak, "Thank you."

"Is the pain down low?" Jael reached over to rub Hava's back just below her waist. "About here?"

"Yes."

"It is pressure from the baby. Lying on your side should help a great deal." For a while Jael massaged Hava's back to soothe the strain. When Hava began to breathe evenly again, Jael eased herself back into the chair. Exhaustion quickly overtook her, and she could no longer remain alert. Just as she faded into sleep, a commanding voice shattered the darkness. She bolted upright as the words pierced her soul.

"Wo, wo, wo unto this people except they shall repent, for the devil laugheth and his angels rejoice because of the slain of the fair sons and daughters of my people."

SEVENTEEN

Jael hugged her arms to her chest. The voice seemed to come from everywhere and nowhere—from all around her and yet from within her.

"And it is because of their iniquity and abominations that they are fallen. Behold, that great city Zarahemla have I burned with fire, and the inhabitants thereof. And behold, that great city Moroni have I caused to be sunk in the depths of the sea, and the inhabitants thereof to be drowned."

Jael wrapped her arms over her head to shut out the sound. But the voice continued, detailing other lands and cities which had reaped death and destruction.

Hava began to weep. Jael reached out and discovered Hava's body in a spasm of sobs. Fearing the effect on the unborn child, Jael moved to the edge of the bed where she could enfold Hava in her arms. Together they huddled as the voice echoed through the blackness.

"O all ye that are spared because ye were more righteous than they, will ye not now return unto me, and repent of your sins, and be converted, that I may heal you?"

Tears stung Jael's eyes. She tried to blink them away. But each word seemed a sharp sword, jabbing at her heart. Then, in her arms, Hava's body convulsed in pain. Though Jael clasped her more tightly, Hava rocked and wailed.

Still the voice persisted. Amidst Hava's cries, Jael heard only part of what was spoken. *"Behold, I am Jesus Christ, the Son of God. . . . I am the light and the life of the world. . . . Behold, I have come unto the world to bring redemption unto the world, to save the world from sin. . . . Therefore, whoso repenteth and cometh unto me as a little child, him will I receive, for of such is the king-dom of God."*

Then, just as mysteriously as it began, the voice ended. Jael continued to clutch Hava's writhing form. Her travail seemed to go on forever. Jael felt powerless to do anything. Tears spilled from her eyes. All she could think of was the commanding voice and its message. Surely it was the voice of Jesus Christ. And surely, as He had said the kingdom of God was made of children, He must be mindful of the imminent birth of Hava's baby. "Oh, please, Dear Lord!" Jael bowed her head to ask for peace and wisdom to see them through this dark hour. Within seconds, Hava stopped moaning.

With the back of one hand, Jael wiped the moisture from her own eyes. Then she lay Hava down on the bed and once again rubbed her back. "What more can I do to help?"

"Water," Hava whispered.

"You want me to sponge your face with water?"

"No," she said weakly. "There is water on the bed. The baby has pushed it forth from me."

Jael's throat constricted. For a moment she could not make herself speak. Instead, she smoothed the straggles of hair from Hava's face. Finally she remembered the words her mother said at such a time. "This is a good sign, Hava. It means you are nearing the end of your travail."

Jael stood and reached toward the head of the bed to locate the bands of cloth, driven into the wall by sturdy wooden pegs. She yanked on the bands to test their strength. Hava began to moan once more.

"Is another pain beginning?"

"Yes!" Hava cried.

"Reach over your head and take hold of these bands of cloth." Jael helped Hava's trembling hands get a firm grip. "Now pull on the bands, take in a deep breath, and try to bear down with the pain."

Hava inhaled raggedly. A guttural noise began deep in her throat. The sound grew more and more intense until it ripened into a piercing shriek.

Jael clenched her fists so tightly that her nails dug into her palms. She felt as if Hava's agony were her own. Then she recalled what Mother did after such an acute pain: check the position of the baby.

Laying her hand on Hava's swollen abdomen, Jael waited until the contraction of muscles ceased. "You are doing well, Hava. Micah would be proud of you." Jael let her fingers probe, trying to understand how the baby lay inside the womb. But Hava's skirts were too thick. And yet another contraction began. "Pull against the bands of cloth," Jael reminded her. "Take a deep—"

Hava screamed. Jael wanted to flee from the room. But she forced her hands to remain on Hava's abdomen. As the muscles tightened, Jael sensed the downward push of the baby. "Good, Hava, bear down."

Hava's wailing gradually subsided. Jael said softly, "It is time to take off your skirts. The birth is drawing near, and I must check how the baby is doing."

"My skirts are wet anyway."

For a moment, their hands worked in unison: untying, unwrapping, and removing the layers of skirting. Then Hava sank back with a tattered sigh. Moments later the pains began anew. Jael wrung out the cloth and sponged the woman's face and neck. Then she remembered that she must wash Hava, as was the custom of purification, in preparation for the birth. And she did not know where in the darkness to find the cleansing herbs.

Jael made her way to the adjoining room and knelt at Esther's bedside. "Mother? Are you all right?"

"Oh, Jael," Esther's voice rasped with sleepiness.

"Hava is nearing the end of her travail."

"Then I must come and assist you."

Jael's heart wrenched as she touched the fevered brow. So many things could go wrong if she tried to deliver this baby alone. But it would weaken Mother more to come and help. "Rest a while longer. I shall call you when I need your help."

Esther found Jael's hand. "I am blessed to have such a daughter as you."

Jael longed to stay at Mother's bedside, but Hava's moans began again. "Where are the birthing basket and other supplies?"

"To your left, on the table in the corner."

Jael located what she needed and went back to Hava. Placing the large, shallow basket on the floor, she laid a clean cloth in it. She poured some vinegar in a bowl, then, one by one, she sniffed the small clay pots until she found the astringent herbs. She sprinkled some of the dried plants into the bowl of vinegar and stirred it with her fingers. She then squeezed the pungent-smelling liquid through the cloth. "Hava, forgive me for using cold vinegar, but that is all I have until we can light a fire."

Hava flinched as the cold cloth contacted her flesh. Jael apologized once more as she washed the woman's abdomen, then she began on her thighs. Cramping pangs began, causing Hava to draw up her knees. "Grasp the bands and bear down," said Jael, rushing to finish the washing. As Hava strained, Jael felt the protruding wet head of the baby.

"Mother!" Jael called as panic gripped her. "Mother, I need you! Please come. It is time."

Jael dropped the damp cloth back in the bowl. "Hava, I am going to try to turn the baby's head so you can push the shoulders out." She struggled to make her fingers work despite the slippery flesh. Hava ceased straining and Jael noticed the head had not come much further forth. Then she sensed Esther at her side. "Mother, I think she would be better squatting when the next pain comes."

Esther leaned over Hava. "I am pleased with what you have done, Jael. The baby is in a good position. Hava, you are nearly through. I believe it is best for you to move off the bed for the birth. Jael will help you."

"First, slide your legs off the edge until your feet touch the floor." Jael tucked her arms under Hava's knees and struggled to lift her legs. As she swung Hava's feet to the floor, a muscle pulled in her own back. Jael set her jaw against the pain and went on with her work. She anchored both hands under Hava's shoulders and raised her up.

"I am somewhat useless with my broken wrist," Esther said. "But I shall try to help by sitting on the edge of the bed. Hava, you crouch in front of me and wrap your arms around my legs. Jael will place the birthing basket beneath you and help to draw the baby forth."

Jael nearly let go of Hava. Never before had she done more than support the woman from behind. Her hands jittered as she eased Hava into a squatting position. She shook her head, trying to throw off the dark fears that saturated her mind like the mists of darkness around her.

The waves of pain returned. Hava lurched and groaned. Jael slid the basket between the woman's feet. She worked rapidly to free the baby from between Hava's straining thighs. Then everything happened at once: the slippery form plunging into her hands, the squirming vigor of the small body, the smell of warm blood and body fluids, and the long shuddering sigh from Hava.

Jael hung the tiny baby over one arm and gently swept a finger through its mouth to release any residual fluid. The child gagged, coughed, and let out a sudden cry. Then Jael ran her hands over every inch of the sleek flesh. She carefully probed each tiny facial feature. She counted toes and fingers. Finally she held the baby towards the new mother. "You have a son, Hava.

He is well and whole. Praise the Lord!"

After that, everything happened in a haze. Jael eased Hava through the afterpains, cleansed the child and mother, and tucked both of them, as well as her own mother, back into bed.

At the table, she ate more bread and honey in an effort to renew her strength. But soon, she folded her arms on the table and lay her head upon them. Sleep came quickly and deeply and was strewn with troubled dreams. But her awakening was more troubled. The thundering voice returned, all around her and yet within her. It took a moment for her groggy mind to grasp the words.

"O ye house of Israel whom I have spared, how oft will I gather you as a hen gathereth her chickens under her wings, if ye will repent and return unto me with full purpose of heart."

Jael raised her head and discovered a hand on her shoulder. "Did you hear what was said?" Mother asked.

"Yes, most of it. A voice with such power that it weakens my soul, and yet at the same time, it gives me strength." Jael heard the new baby whimper in the corner. "Is there something I can do, Hava?"

"No, Jael, we are fine. He is learning to nurse."

Jael brushed strands of hair off her face. "Mother, should you be out of bed?"

"I had to get up when I heard the voice." Esther sat in a chair beside Jael. "I shall abide here for a time and rest."

"Did you hear the voice before, when you were asleep?"

"I thought it was merely part of my dreams. This time I know it came from heaven."

"But what does it mean? 'Gather you as a hen gathereth her chickens under her wings.'"

"We shall ask my brother Nephi when next we see him."

Jael heard the baby sucking. What a miracle: a new life, coming from the depths of this darkness. And Jesus Christ would also come after the darkness dispersed. "Mother, I forgot to tell you what Uncle Nephi said." Jael ran her fingernails along the woven strands of her wool dress. "He has asked that everyone assemble at the temple. It is prophesied that sometime after the light returns, Jesus Christ will come and visit us."

"I fear I am too weary to abide His coming."

"Remember the voice while you were sleeping? It was the voice of Jesus Christ, saying that those of us still alive were spared because we were more righteous. Then He promised that if we will turn to Him and repent, He will heal us. Oh, Mother, I believe with all my heart that He can heal you and make you whole again."

"Your faith has been strengthened in these mists of darkness."

"Yes. I understand more about the workings of the Spirit." Jael clutched her hands to her breast. "When I was alone in the darkness, the only guide I had was the Light of Christ within me. And now I know I can have that Light forever in my life, if only I seek after it." Stretching her hands overhead, Jael shook off her fatigue and sat up straight. "Mother, listen."

"Is it the voice again?"

"No, listen. It is a quieter sound."

"Oh, Jael! The birds are chirping."

"Just as they always have before the light dawns!" Jael went toward the door, swung it open wide, and stepped out into the garden. She looked toward the heavens. A faint glow appeared behind the distant hills to the east. Her hands shot upward, welcoming the restored light. And slowly she pirouetted, drinking in the freshness of a new day.

Then Jael dropped to her knees in the storm-battered garden. Head bowed and hands folded calmly in her lap, she breathed a prayer of thanks to the Lord for seeing her through the mists of darkness. Warmth wrapped like a quilt around her shoulders. Never before had she felt so close to God. Her soul lifted to such heights that she expected to be floating when she opened her eyes.

After a moment, Jael stood up and gazed at the renewing light. Dim forms of pastel clouds now cushioned the eastern hills. Though she longed to linger until all the heavens were illuminated, she could not wait to share the joy with Mother and rushed back inside. "The darkness is over. Light is peeking over the eastern hills!"

"Hosanna!" Esther praised.

"Hosanna!" echoed Hava across the room.

"Hosanna! Blessed be the name of the Most High God!" Jael began singing, and the other women joined in. "Hosanna! Blessed be the name of the Almighty God!"

EIGHTEEN

"Jael?" a young voice called through the open doorway. "Micah sent me to see about Hava."

"Oh, Sarah!" Jael rushed to embrace her. "Forgive me. I meant to come speak with you. But I was so tired after the birth that I fell asleep."

"Then Hava is all right?"

"She is the mother of a magnificent son! Come and see." Jael smiled. "As yet it is barely light enough to see him. But is it not a blessing that the darkness is fading?"

"Yes!" Sarah followed Jael across the room. "May I hold the baby?"

"Here, sit beside me on the bed." Hava reached out with the bundled baby. Jael took the child and laid him in Sarah's arms.

"He is so small!" Sarah said.

"I am glad he was small," Hava smiled. "Now someone must go and tell Micah about his son."

"I promised to return quickly." Sarah handed the child back to his mother.

Jael walked Sarah to the door and waved her off to get Micah. Then she turned and surveyed the room in the faint light. "It looks as though the house could use some tidying after the storm and earthquakes." Mother began to rise from her chair, but Jael laid a hand on her shoulder. "No, Mother, I shall do the cleaning while you continue to rest. But first I must try something."

At the woodpile beside the hearth, Jael snapped twigs and shredded bark. Then she struck a pair of stones together. Sparks caught hold on the kindling, and soon the hearth danced with flames of warmth and light.

Mother came to stand nearby. "Jael, you are a young woman full of miracles: finding your way through the mists of darkness, midwifing a baby, and now building a fire when no one else could."

"With the darkness fading, everyone shall again be able to build fires." Jael kissed her mother's cheek. Then she hoisted a large clay pot and went toward the door. "Now, sit down and rest while I get water from the river for cleaning."

Jael went out to behold the increasing dawn of light. She made a quick survey of her homeland. Countless trees had fallen and many homes were shattered. She went around to the back of her house, where the huge tree sprawled up the embankment. How much of her world had been ravaged! What a blessing the darkness had hidden it all from view until now.

For a moment, she set down the clay pot. Then she noticed her sandal with Mathoni's headband tied around it. Both joy and sadness washed over her, as strong as currents in the river. She hugged her arms to her chest and leaned back against a branch of the fallen tree. It seemed so long ago that Mathoni had held her, yet it could not have been more than eight or ten hours. Since then, so much had changed—within her and around her. Even the course of the river seemed different, with the new pool of water beside the fallen tree.

Her eyes followed the tree trunk down to the upturned roots. Something moved in the river behind the roots. Suddenly a man charged out of the current. A glimmer of light reflected off his face. Mathoni!

Jael's knees buckled. She grabbed onto a branch. Her every thought beckoned her to sprint down the embankment. But she had only the strength to hold onto the branch and gape. She watched Mathoni wade into the pool, lie down, and scrub his fingers through his hair—cleansing himself as she had earlier. Soon he got up and shook the moisture from his arms.

Then he raised his head. Instantly he saw Jael and sloshed out of the pool. She caught her breath. Before she could think to calm her racing heart, he had clambered up the embankment and stood, dripping, before her. She clung mightily to the branch and stared at him wide-eyed.

"Hah! Do your eyes not believe what they see?"

"I . . . I," Jael let go of the branch and reached toward him.

"So you want to touch me and see if I am real?" He held out his arms. "But I must warn you, I am drenched."

Jael did not care. She fell into his arms and soaked up every bit of him she could. Even with the moisture, she felt warmer in his grasp than ever before.

Then, over his shoulder, she saw a shaft of sunlight strike the trees across the river. Within seconds, sunshine filled the air around them. Pulling slightly away, Jael blinked at the brightness. Mathoni grinned, showing his white teeth. Glistening water droplets shone like jewels in his dark hair. As she gazed into his intensely-green eyes, his left eyebrow raised.

He kissed her forehead. "You are a lovely sight to behold after three days of darkness."

"Oh, Mathoni!" His name felt like honey on her tongue. She could not keep from repeating it. "Mathoni, Mathoni. Praise the Lord! He has led you back to me in safety. But what of your sister? And where are Jonas and Uncle Ti . . ."

"Hush, now." Mathoni gently laid a finger against her lips. "All is well. The Lord has been merciful. I have witnessed His power and beheld many miracles. Someday I shall share it all with you." His hand moved to rest against her cheek. "Someday I hope to share the whole of my life with you."

Jael laid her head against his wet vest and tunic.

"What a vision you were, standing beside this fallen tree."

"I meant to get water to clean the house."

"Let me help you." Mathoni released her and reached down for the clay pot.

Jael watched each simple movement as he walked to the pool, filled the pot, and returned to her side. "Please, Mathoni, I must know about your sister."

"Martha was one of several trapped in the fallen storehouse. When we freed her and others, I did what I could in the darkness to ease their pain. Martha's pelvis was broken and her abdomen had swollen, perhaps from bleeding or infection. She was unconscious and near death. There seemed little I could do." Mathoni took in a deep breath and glanced skyward for a moment. "But through the power of God's priesthood, Martha will make a full recovery. Timothy and Jonas laid their hands on her head, and within minutes she was awake and said she felt very little pain. Before I left, she was taking small amounts of broth."

"And the others who were trapped?"

"Also miraculously saved."

"The Lord truly has been merciful." Jael barely felt the ground beneath her feet as they circled to the front of the house. When they entered, she saw the startled expression on Esther's face. "Mother, this is Mathoni, son of Zedekiah the physician."

"Your traveling companion in the darkness?"

"Jonas was also with us," Mathoni hastened to say.

Jael lowered her head to conceal the rush of blood to her cheeks. "Mother, I had hoped Mathoni could ease the pain in your wrist."

"How did you hurt it?" he asked.

"I fell during the earthquakes. I believe it is broken. Perhaps you would examine it for me?"

"It would be an honor." Mathoni knelt beside Esther and carefully probed the injured forearm. "Yes, the bones are misaligned, and the flesh here is red and swollen. There are two bones in this part of your arm, yet it appears that you have broken but one of the two."

"Does that mean I—" Esther could not finish because of the coughing that racked her body.

"You should have stayed in bed," said Jael, laying her hands on Mother's shoulders. "Mathoni, this disease of the lungs has plagued her far too long. We must find a cure."

Mathoni looked into Esther's face. "I can easily splint your wrist and soothe the pain there. But may I suggest a better healer than I for your lungs?"

"Your father?" asked Jael.

"Not my earthly father, though he is a worthy physician." Mathoni's voice softened. "There is a powerful Healer that I have recently come to know. During the final hours of darkness, I heard the voice of the Lord Jesus Christ. He said if we would return to Him and be converted that He would heal us."

Jael knelt beside Mathoni and laid her hand on his. "I, too, heard His voice and believe in His power to heal."

Mathoni gazed out the door at the bright sunlight. Moisture glistened in the corners of his eyes. "I have witnessed for myself His power to heal. Not only does He heal people of their physical wounds and make them whole," Mathoni blinked back tears, "but I shall never forget how God reached into my soul, healed my wounded spirit, and made me whole."

Jael laid her cheek against his arm. When she had prayed earlier, she experienced the same healing within her soul, yet she did not know how to put it into words.

Mathoni took in a deep breath. "No longer will I see death as my greatest foe. In the future, when I treat those who are sick or wounded, I believe that even if they die, I will have saved them, if I can but heal their spiritual wounds."

Jael nodded against his arm. So much peace and gratitude filled her that she could not speak.

Mathoni stood and gently brought Jael to her feet. Then he glanced across the room to see Hava on the bed and Micah sitting close by. Mathoni's left eyebrow shot up. "I did not realize there were others in the house."

"Hava has just delivered a son," Esther explained. "Jael proved to be a fine midwife."

"Hava is the one who should be praised," Jael responded.

Mathoni pulled her to his side. "Perhaps you would assist me in splinting your mother's wrist? A cool, damp cloth would ease the swelling."

Jael smiled up at him, then went to dip a cloth in the basin of water. She laid the cloth upon her mother's arm while Mathoni searched the woodpile for smooth twigs. Then together they made a splint and sling for Esther's wrist.

Micah came forward with the tiny child in his arms. Mathoni admired the baby and gave honor to the parents.

"Where is Sarah?" asked Jael.

"Hava sent her home to gather some things for the baby," said Micah. "As our firstborn son, we must soon go to present him at the temple."

"You shall not be going alone," announced Mathoni. "I have been asked to gather everyone in this quarter of the land and lead them to the temple. Timothy has already sent numerous companies on their way."

Jael glanced at her mother.

Esther sat up straighter in her chair. "Perhaps with one of Micah's wagons, I could also make the journey."

"It is the least I could give in return for your help in the birth of my son."

"Are you eager to leave right away?" asked Jael.

"I am." Mathoni laid an arm across her shoulders. "Though no one is certain when the Lord will appear, I want to make sure we are at the temple when He comes."

"Yes," Jael nodded as a sense of wonder tingled through her. "There is nothing more important in our lives than beholding Jesus Christ, the Savior and Redeemer of the World."

About the Author

Bonnie Robinson is a native of Salt Lake City, where she lives with her husband, Glenn, and their four children. The Robinsons love the outdoors—summers in the mountains biking, hiking, and camping, where Bonnie likes playing her guitar and singing by the campfire; winters cross-country and downhill skiing. A graduate of Utah State University, Bonnie does calligraphy, gathers flowers and weeds to make wreaths and other crafts.